Burning Bright

Also by Sophie McKenzie

Burning Bright

SOPHIE McKENZIE

SIMON AND SCHUSTER

Acknowledgments: with thanks to Moira Young, Gaby Halberstam,
Julie Mckenzie, Melanie Edge, Lou Kuenzler and Lily Kuenzler.

First published in Great Britain in 2013 by Simon
and Schuster UK Ltd, a CBS company.

The right of Sophie McKenzie to be identified as the author of
this work has been asserted by her in accordance with sections
77 and 78 of the Copyright, Design and Patents Act, 1988.

Simon & Schuster UK Ltd
1st Floor, 222 Gray's Inn Road, London WC1X 8HB

A CIP catalogue record for this book is available from the British Library.

PB ISBN: 978-0-85707-101-9
EBOOK ISBN: 978-0-85707-102-6

1 3 5 7 9 10 8 6 4 2

Printed and bound by CPI Group (UK) Ltd, Croydon CR0 4YY.

www.simonandschuster.co.uk
www.sophiemckenziebooks.com

For Jez, Alex and Daisy Startup

1

Emmi banged on the door of my changing cubicle.

'River,' she yelled. 'Come *on*.'

I gritted my teeth and opened the door. Emmi stood in front of me, her hands on her hips. Tall, dark and impatient, the strings of her dark blue designer bikini were looped in artfully casual bows over her slim hips and tanned shoulders. Grace hovered beside her – all fragile and blonde – in a pretty, pink one-piece.

'About time.' Emmi rolled her eyes. 'Everyone else is outside already.'

'Are you okay, Riv?' Grace asked anxiously.

'I can't go,' I stammered, looking down at my plain black swimsuit. 'I look awful.'

'No. You look nice.' Grace smiled at me.

'Forget nice,' Emmi snorted. 'You look hot.'

I stared at her, unconvinced.

'Oh for goodness sake.' Emmi practically stamped

her foot, then dragged me across the damp tiles of the changing room to the low counter with the hairdryers chained to the walls. She spun me round so I was facing the nearest mirror.

'Look,' she snapped. 'Look at the way you curve: Boobs. Waist. Bum. You're *all* curves, Riv. It's sexy.'

I stared at my reflection. At my straggly hair and ditchwater-grey eyes. Then down to my knees. I hated my knees. 'I look short,' I wailed. 'And dumpy.'

'I give up.' Emmi grabbed my arm. 'Fine. You look short and dumpy. You're coming outside anyway.'

And she dragged me through the chlorinated foot bath and through the swing door into the main pool area.

It was a pool party. Alex, Emmi's boyfriend, was seventeen today and Emmi had persuaded him he should celebrate by getting his parents to hire the swimming baths for a couple of hours. That kind of expense is nothing to Emmi. She's loaded. So's Alex – at least he's always flashing his money around. His parents bought him *and* all his brothers an iPad each for Christmas.

Anyway, it was the end of January and had been snowing since yesterday. Kind of an odd time for a party at the swimming baths, but it was typical of Emmi to suggest something that nobody was expecting – and that captured everybody's imagination. Her plan was that we should splash about for a bit, then go for a pizza.

The main pool area was loud with excited chatter. Alex and his friends were gathered on one side with a big posse of girls opposite. Emmi dropped my arm and sashayed towards the boys. I scuttled self-consciously behind her, Grace at my side. Emmi went straight up to Alex and slid a sinuous arm around his middle.

'Happy birthday, babe,' she breathed.

You could practically see Alex's chest puffing up with pride as all his friends stared enviously at Emmi. I backed away and slid into the pool as quickly as I could, relieved to be able to hide my body under the water.

Soon Grace's boyfriend – James Malloy – turned up along with more of Alex and Emmi's friends. Most of the boys were now in the water, mucking about or chatting to the girls. Everyone was shouting or laughing. Having a great time.

I swam a couple of lengths, careful to avoid the noisy male wrestling matches that were going on down one side of the pool. Honestly, they were taking up half the water. And why did they have to be so loud? A large group of girls was watching them – throwing out the occasional comment. My irritation increased. How idiotic did *they* look? All big-eyed and giggling over the stupid wrestling boys. I guess it was really only a typical party. I just wasn't in the mood for all these people. There was only one person I wanted to see. And he wasn't here.

Flynn.

Flynn's my boyfriend. We've been going out for four months, since we met acting in *Romeo and Juliet* at Flynn's school. Emmi says he's trouble. So does my mum. But he's really just kind of intense.

'Oy, River.'

I looked up. I'd been swimming so intently towards the deep end that I hadn't noticed Emmi walking along the edge of the pool beside me.

'What the hell are you doing?' Emmi waved her arms in exasperation. 'This is a party and you look like you're in training for a race.'

I trod water for a moment, gazing up at her. 'I'm fine,' I said.

Emmi grinned and shook her head at me. Alex appeared at her side, tugging at her arm. Emmi winked as she let Alex drag her away.

'He'll be here soon, River. Don't worry.'

I glanced up at the big clock that hung on the wall above the spectator seats. It was almost six. Flynn was still working – he does loads of jobs outside school, trying to help his mum by earning money.

4

Today he'd agreed to finish early so we could enjoy the party together.

I reached the deep end and turned round to swim another length. There were so many people in the pool now that I had to keep stopping and swimming around them. I nodded every time I passed someone I knew, but I didn't stay and talk. There was only one person I wanted to speak to.

I lay in the shallow end for a while, watching my legs drifting about under the water. Then I slid lower in the water and leaned my head back until I was floating. I closed my eyes and reached my arms behind me to the shallow groove in the pool wall. My ears were underwater. I could feel the vibrations of people shrieking and splashing. They all sounded so far away.

Hands grabbed me around my waist. I flailed out with my arms and legs, trying to resist, but the hands holding me were too strong. They pulled me upright, steadying me while I found my feet on the bottom of the pool.

It was Flynn. He stood in front of me, his hands still on my waist.

'You look like a mermaid,' he said with a grin.

I smiled back. It was like the whole world had been in black and white and now it was in colour. Even the party around us was transformed. The noisy boys wrestling along the far side of the pool were just having a laugh, while the girls watching them and giggling seemed charming – not stupid at all.

I drew away to look at him. Flynn's tall. Well, tall compared to me anyway. Long and lean and really muscular. I stared at his beautifully toned arms and his fantastically fit stomach. He looked amazing. It's from all the boxing training he does. It's a big thing to him, working out, though I've never really understood why he feels such a strong need to keep in shape. It's certainly not that he's vain.

Flynn was wearing long dark red swimming trunks. They looked great against his skin.

'Where did you get those?' I asked. 'James?'

Flynn nodded. Well, that was no surprise. Flynn didn't have many clothes and those he did own were mostly second-hand and scruffy. He wouldn't accept a loan off many people but James Molloy, aka Grace's boyfriend, was his best friend.

To be honest, sometimes I wondered if he wasn't Flynn's only friend.

'They look good,' I said.

Flynn pulled me towards him again. 'So do you,' he murmured. I shivered at the low, sexy note in his voice and closed my eyes, ready for his kiss.

6

A tidal wave splashed up over my face. I staggered back, choking, rubbing my eyes. I couldn't breathe. There was water up my nose. Ugh. Laughter broke out around me. I forced my eyes open, though they stung, thanks to the chlorine. Three boys I vaguely recognised from Flynn's class were standing to my right, doubled over with laughter. Had *they* splashed me? No, they were pointing to where the water was churning violently, a few metres away. As I watched, two bodies rose up, out of the waves. Alex and Flynn. Everyone was yelling. Flynn's mouth was open, gasping for air, as he swung his fists at Alex's face. But Alex was too quick. With a roar he ducked Flynn's punch, then reared up and shoved Flynn under the water again.

'Stop!' I yelled.

But the noise in the swimming pool was deafening. I couldn't even hear myself. Heart pounding, I waded towards Flynn. Alex's muscles bulged with the effort of keeping him under. I had to stop him. The water around them was roiling. Panic gripped me. If I didn't reach Flynn soon, he would surely drown.

2

I stretched out my arms, ready to push Alex away from Flynn, but, just as I reached them, Flynn reared up, out of the water. With a bloodcurdling yell he sprang out of Alex's grip, then launched himself forward. Both hands outstretched, Flynn pushed Alex so hard that he flew in an arc over the water, splashing down heavily several metres away.

Alex surfaced, spluttering and swearing his head off. He glared at Flynn, his eyes full of hate, but he stayed where he was.

The shouts and the laughter around us died. The only noise was the sound of Flynn's jagged breathing, and the soft slap of the waves against the pool lining.

Flynn blinked the water out of his eyes. He stared at Alex, then turned to me.

'Are you all right?' he said.

I nodded, still confused. Clearly Alex had splashed me, and Flynn had rushed to my defence, but why had Alex deliberately provoked him like that?

Clenching his fists, Flynn took a step towards Alex through the water. I tensed. So did everyone else around the pool.

Flynn took another step. My chest tightened. He was going to hit Alex again – only much harder this time. An expression of fear shot through Alex's eyes, then a mask of contempt. He drew himself up and pointed at Flynn's clenched fist.

'You sure you want to do that?' he snarled. 'Remember what happened yesterday . . . you know, at school, during the snowstorm?'

Flynn hesitated. His eyes flickered over to me.

I frowned. What was Alex talking about? 'What happened yesterday?'

'Oh, doesn't River know?' Alex said, his voice all mock concern.

'Shut up,' Flynn snapped. He turned to me. 'Don't listen to him.'

'Oh, what's the matter? Lost your nerve?' Alex said. He folded his arms. 'You were happy to lash out before. You have a serious problem.'

This was so unfair, I couldn't keep quiet. 'Stop it,' I said, my voice shaking with anger. 'Flynn didn't do anything to provoke you. We were together and you just came over and—'

'Flynn doesn't need a reason to lose it,' Alex said nastily. 'Like I said, he's got a serious problem – and it's not just the violence.'

I stared at him. What was Alex talking about? I was beside Flynn now. Flynn was glaring at Alex, his whole body tensed with rage. Any second now he was going to lose his temper properly. I'd seen him hit people before and I knew that shove he'd given Alex before was nothing compared to what he was capable of.

'It's time to get out now anyway,' Emmi said, materialising at the poolside just above Alex's head. 'Come on, babe.'

Alex glanced up at her and Flynn turned away.

'We'll get out when we're ready,' Flynn spat.

Alex gave a disgusted snort. 'You know you're only here because of *her*.' He pointed to me. 'If she wasn't Emmi's best friend . . .' With a shake of his head, Alex hauled himself out of the pool. As he stalked off towards the changing rooms I caught Emmi's eye. She looked relieved – but also embarrassed. The people watching the scene were drifting away – the boys who'd been laughing before, started splashing at each other. Noise rose up, echoing off the swimming bath walls. It was over.

'Come on, River,' Flynn said. He splashed noisily across the pool.

I hesitated. It wasn't nice to hear Flynn was only at the party because Alex felt he *had* to invite him, though I wasn't surprised. But what really bothered me was Alex's reference to Flynn's 'problem'. What exactly was he talking about? I had the strong sense that Emmi knew, just like Flynn did, but that neither of them wanted me to find out. Emmi turned to follow Alex.

'Wait, Emmi,' I said, pulling myself half out of the water.

She stopped. Turned back to face me. Her expression was guarded.

'What did Alex mean when he said Flynn's problem "wasn't just the violence"?' I asked. 'What did Flynn do yesterday that made Alex attack him just now?'

Emmi shrugged. 'No idea.' She walked away into the changing rooms. A shiver ran down my spine. She was lying, I was sure. But why?

All over the pool, people were emerging, dripping, from the water. I slid back in and swam over to Flynn. By the time I reached him, we were the only two people left. A few minutes ago that would have seemed romantic but the magic of the moment when Flynn found me had gone and I was only aware of how cold the water was, full of stinky chlorine, making my skin pucker. Flynn was treading water in the deep end, his face still thunderous. I took a deep breath. I knew from experience, asking Flynn difficult questions at the wrong moment was likely to make him explode.

'About what happened yesterday . . .' I began.

'It was just Alex trying to wind me up, okay?' he snapped. 'I don't want to talk about it.'

'Right.' I was sure there was more to what had happened than that, but equally aware there was no point pushing Flynn right now. 'Shall we get out?'

Flynn's face relaxed. 'In a second.' He put his hands back on my face. 'You look so beautiful.' His eyes were sparkling, so intently focused on me that I felt my neck and face above the water burning. Flynn thought I was gorgeous. Which meant that, surely, I must at least look better than I'd thought. The water was bringing out the emerald in his green-gold eyes. He ducked lower in the water, so it lapped against his chin, then he pulled me right up against him. I forgot where I was as he kissed me. His kisses were perfect – hard but soft, pushing, yet pulling – always listening to the way I kissed him back.

I ran my hands up his wet, smooth back. My fingers reached his shoulders and I felt the jagged line of the scar where his da had glassed him. He told everyone else it was a scar from a fight. I was the only person who knew the truth – that his family have no money and his dad's a violent drunk who's not supposed to come near Flynn or his mum or sisters.

'We should go,' I said.

'I'll just swim a couple of lengths first,' Flynn said. 'See you outside?'

I nodded and Flynn splashed away. I watched as he got into his stride, hurtling furiously down the pool. Despite our kiss, it was obvious he was still angry – you could see it in every pull of his arms, every kick of his legs. All my previous anxieties surged back. What was Flynn so mad about? What 'serious problem' had Alex been talking about before? And what had happened yesterday?

I got out and trudged, alone, to the changing rooms.

3

I showered and changed into my jeans, still puzzling over what Alex had said. Maybe I was overreacting. Maybe Alex was just trying to wind Flynn up. They didn't like each other, after all. The tension between them had started because of Emmi: just before Christmas, Emmi had played Juliet in the play at the boys' school. Flynn had been Romeo and I know Alex had wondered – like I had done – whether Emmi and Flynn had enjoyed kissing each other in the play more than they let on. I knew now that my fears had been groundless but, even though Alex must know this too, it was clear he had disliked Flynn ever since.

I pulled my top over my head and hurried out of the cubicle, determined to find Emmi as soon as possible and force her to tell me what she knew. But there was no sign of her. In fact the changing room was almost empty. I scurried over to the hairdryers to dry my hair. Grace was already there, tugging a comb through her sleek blonde bob.

'Hey, Grace,' I said casually. 'I was just wondering. Did James tell you anything that happened at the guys' school yesterday? Something to do with Flynn? During the snowstorm?'

Grace blinked round at me. 'What?' she said. 'Why?'

I told her what had just happened by the pool.

Grace blushed. 'Oh, Riv . . .' She stopped.

'What?'

'Well.' Grace squirmed. 'James did say something earlier . . . about Flynn getting into a fight at school yesterday afternoon. He pushed some boy into a hedge or something.'

I nodded. It wasn't the first time Flynn had been in a fight. He'd never hurt me – or made me feel scared that he might – but I'd seen him fly off the handle at the slightest provocation. It was hard to predict when it was going to happen, so many things made him angry.

'What was the fight about?' I asked, still confused as to why either Flynn or Emmi would want to keep the details from me – and why, in particular, Alex mentioning it just now had stopped Flynn from hitting him.

Grace looked across the changing room. I got the

strong impression she didn't want to look me in the eyes, much like Emmi earlier. 'Grace?' I said.

'Didn't Flynn tell you *any* of this?' Grace bit her lip. 'God, James is gonna kill me.'

'So what happened?' I said, not knowing whether to feel more angry or bewildered. 'Why the big secret?'

'I don't know the whole story.' Grace took my hand. Hers felt warm. I realised I was shivering. 'James just said the fight was over a girl.'

'A *girl*?' The words came out of me in a tiny voice. After all my suspicions at the end of last term, that Flynn really liked Emmi, I'd convinced myself he was totally into me. Okay, so we hadn't gone as far as most of the couples I knew, but Flynn was cool with that. At least I thought he was.

'James didn't know the details,' Grace went on. 'It was . . . Flynn had upset someone's girlfriend and the guy had a go at him. James didn't think it was a big deal . . . Flynn's *always* upsetting people. You know that.'

'Upset her how?' I asked.

'I don't know,' Grace stammered.

'Right.' I felt numb. There could be loads of explanations for what Flynn had done. But why didn't he want me to know about it? Why had Alex's mention of it in front of me made him back away?

16

Grace turned her attention back to the mirror, applying a little eyeshadow and a dash of pale pink lipgloss. Unlike Emmi, who favoured dark, dramatic make-up, Grace usually went for a completely natural look.

'That's pretty,' I said, indicating the lipgloss.

Grace glanced sideways and offered me a shy smile. 'Thanks, Riv. Er, are you okay?'

'Sure.' I stroked mascara onto my eyelashes, trying to put what I'd just heard out of my head.

Grace shuffled from foot to foot.

'I'll see you outside,' I said.

'Okay.' She sounded relieved.

Alone in the changing room, I took my time brushing my hair and putting on the rest of my make-up. Why did everything with Flynn always have to be so complicated?

I trusted him.

I loved him.

He barely had to touch me before I was off my head, totally overwhelmed with how much I wanted him back.

It was terrifying how much I felt for him.

Which of course was part of the problem. It all mattered so much – what he did, what he said, how he felt about me.

Somehow, when I was around Flynn, it was all

17

too easy to lose myself: to feel that all I was, was reflected in his eyes. Like being with him was a brighter, sharper reality than everything else in my life.

By the time I got outside the swimming baths, everyone apart from Flynn was already halfway up the road. He smiled when he saw me, his breath misting into the chilly night air. Most of the snow from yesterday's storm had melted now, but it was still really cold.

'What were you doing in there?' he said.

'Thinking.'

Flynn hesitated. 'Thinking that maybe we didn't have to go for this stupid pizza with everyone?'

I stared at him. 'It was only *Alex* being a jerk,' I said.

Flynn rolled his eyes. 'It's Alex's party.'

'What happened yesterday?' I said. Images were now flashing through my head: Flynn flirting with someone's girlfriend . . . Flynn holding *her* by the waist, looking into *her* eyes, kissing *her* lips . . .

'I told you – nothing,' Flynn growled.

'But it wasn't nothing, was it?' I said. 'You got in a fight yesterday at school, during the snowstorm. You pushed some boy into a hedge because he was angry with you. *That* was what Alex was talking about before, wasn't it?'

Flynn met my gaze. He said nothing, but the sullen look in his eyes told me that I was right.

'The boy you pushed was mad with you over some girl?' I said, anxiety now knotting my guts.

'Who told you that?' Flynn snapped.

'It doesn't matter,' I said, tears threatening to well up. He wasn't bothering to deny it. 'Who was she? What had you done with her? Why don't you want to tell me about it?'

'It was nothing, nobody was hurt,' Flynn insisted. 'It was just a misunderstanding.'

'Right.' Angry, terrified misery filled me. I turned and stalked up the road after the others. I didn't look round to see if Flynn was following me. What was the point? If he couldn't trust me with whatever had happened, we didn't have much of a relationship anyway.

Flynn caught up with me as I reached Amore Pizza. Everyone else was already inside the restaurant, taking off their coats and finding seats around the long table.

'River?' he said, touching my arm. 'I just don't want to talk about it, right now, okay?'

I shrugged and went inside, feeling hurt and angry. Okay, so Flynn didn't want to talk. Maybe I was overreacting, but what with school and all his jobs, we had so little time together . . . so few opportunities to be close. And he was spoiling what should have been a really nice night.

I deliberately sat apart from him while we were having our pizza. He looked over at me a couple of times, but didn't say anything. Later everyone started getting tanked up on beers and he pulled out some money – I knew it would be the exact money for what he'd eaten. As usual, he couldn't afford to pay a split of the bill, and anyway – because of his da – Flynn never drank alcohol, so he'd have been paying for other people's booze.

Despite the fact that it was fair, I knew that Flynn hated having to do it. I could see his eyes hardening as he left his cash with James. He looked over at me one last time – a long, resentful look. Then he got up and walked away from the table without saying goodbye.

My stomach twisted into knots as I watched him leave. I caught Grace's eye. She was smiling at me sympathetically. Then I looked up the table to where a very drunken Alex was chewing Emmi's face off.

It was crazy. Grace was fond of James. And Emmi certainly fancied Alex. But I was sure neither of them felt like Flynn and I did about each other. So why was it always so difficult with him? Why did he get so angry and moody about everything? Why did I get so upset?

I stood up and stomped out of the restaurant. Everyone would know I'd gone after Flynn, but I didn't care. I wanted to tell him how furious I was. How stupid he was being.

Outside it was still bitterly cold. My breath whirled in front of my face as I glanced up and down the road.

Flynn was leaning against the wall of the bank next to the pizza restaurant looking across at me. His eyes glinted gold in the street lights as he pushed himself off the wall. Then he strolled lazily over, his hands in his pockets, a smile creeping round the edges of his mouth. How annoying! He'd *known* I would follow him outside. He was infuriatingly sure of himself.

And so unbearably sexy that I couldn't look away.

He stopped just in front of me. 'Thanks for coming out,' he said.

'Why are you being so horrible?' I snapped, angry at him for being able to predict my behaviour like that.

Flynn raised his eyebrows. 'I just said I didn't want to talk right now which—'

'I know what you said, but it's not fair. Alex knows. Emmi knows. And it's not my fault Alex wound you up about whatever it is.' I paused. 'The truth is you don't trust me.'

Flynn blinked. He looked genuinely shocked.

'It isn't that, Riv, honest.'

'Then tell me what happened rather than playing these stupid games – walking out and waiting for me to follow you.' A gust of icy wind blew through my top. I shivered, wishing I'd worn a warmer jacket.

Flynn smiled. He put his hands on my arms, warming them. I was turned on. Really turned on. Just by standing next to him. Just by the feel of his hands.

This made me even angrier, mostly with myself.

'I know Alex was an idiot earlier but you're spoiling the whole evening,' I said, shaking off his hands. 'And for what? Why? What's the matter with you?'

I turned away, intending to march back into the restaurant. Flynn grabbed my arm again.

'You're right,' he said. 'I'm sorry. I was going to tell you what happened, but I didn't want to have to think about it and get cross all over again.' He paused. 'I was actually trying *not* to spoil everything tonight.'

I sighed, letting his words sink in, feeling my rage ebb away. This was so typical of my life with Flynn. One minute I'd be full of fury. The next, Flynn would do or say something that stood everything on its head and my anger would evaporate, as if it had never existed.

I let Flynn pull me round to face him. He slid his hands into mine.

'The fight *was* about a girl, but not the way that sounds,' he said in a low voice, his eyes burning into mine. 'You know Café Yazmina?'

'Of course.' Café Yazmina was one of the places Flynn worked.

'Well, one of Alex's friends came in with his girl-friend when I was working there on Thursday night and apparently she lost her purse. The next day Alex and his friend accused me of stealing it. They were totally in my face and I got mad and pushed them away. It's just so typical. Everyone at school always assumes I'm to blame when anything happens.'

'They thought you stole a purse?' I frowned. My head had been so full of images of Flynn making out with another girl that I hadn't stopped to consider he might have got into a fight over something else. It didn't fit with what I knew of him – Flynn might be mouthy and aggressive, but I couldn't imagine him stealing anything.

'It's just an excuse . . . something to attack me with because I don't fit in,' Flynn said.

He sounded full of fight, but I could see the pain in his eyes.

23

'Oh, Flynn,' I said, moving closer to him. 'They've got no proof. Nobody who knows you will listen to rubbish like that, it's just gossip.'

Flynn made a face. 'It's not the first time I've been accused of stealing stuff. You know, things get lost and people at school go behind my back and tell the teachers it was probably me. After a while everyone starts to believe it, even though there's no evidence. And I've been given millions of detentions for my attitude, whatever that means, and for fighting too.' He hesitated. 'After the fight yesterday they called in my mum and said I'd been in trouble too often. They . . . they gave me a one-day exclusion for Monday.'

'No,' I breathed.

Flynn shrugged. 'I mean, I couldn't care less about missing the lessons, but I *have* to get my A levels.' His mouth trembled. 'Otherwise staying on at school will have been a total waste of time.'

I nodded, understanding straight away. Unlike anyone else I knew, Flynn's priority was to look after his mum. He was hoping to get to uni and become a lawyer . . . something that would make people respect him, he'd said, and that paid really well.

We stood looking at each other for a moment. It struck me I'd been silly to get so upset before. I mean, sure, Flynn could have told me all that stuff earlier, but I understood why he hadn't wanted to go into it during the party and, anyway, he'd told me now. His life was so difficult . . . so full of problems I couldn't begin to understand.

I lifted my face up a fraction and Flynn bent down to kiss me. A long, slow, lingering kiss. Goosebumps that had nothing to do with the cold air ridged along my arms.

'So that's why you stopped yourself from punching Alex, because you don't want the school to have any more excuses to have a go at you?'

Flynn shrugged. 'Partly,' he said. 'But also because you were there and I knew you'd hate it.' He smiled, his whole face lighting up, and I felt a sudden rush of love for him. I hugged him hard.

'D'you want to go back in?' Flynn said, pointing through the window to the others inside the restaurant.

I followed his gaze. Emmi was standing by Alex's chair. Two of his friends, clearly drunk, were hanging on her every word. Further down the table James and Grace were deep in conversation. Everyone was chatting and happy.

They didn't need us. We didn't need them.

'No,' I said. 'Let's go back to mine. Mum won't be back till late.'

25

We walked along in silence. Flynn rested his arm across my shoulders. I wound mine round his lean, muscular back and put my head against his chest. I loved how we could walk along like that, fitting perfectly into each other, not needing to say anything.

Everything was perfect.

Well, what happened earlier hadn't been perfect – Flynn had got into an argument at school and been suspended and his tussle with Alex made it harder than ever for all our friends to get on – but he hadn't gone after any other girls.

He was mine.

Totally mine.

4

'See you later, Mum,' I yelled as I charged across the hall the following Saturday. I'd hoped to get away from the house before she stopped me, but she was out of the kitchen and into the hall before I'd even opened the front door.

'Where are you going?' Her eyes narrowed suspiciously. 'I thought we could go out later – do some shopping, spend some time together. I never get to see you properly nowadays.'

'Sorry, Mum.' I shot her an apologetic smile. 'I'm meeting Grace and Emmi,' I lied. 'I'm late, in fact.' I pulled the front door open.

'Well, when will you be back?' Mum's voice was plaintive. Typical. She sometimes spent whole weekends at stupid work conferences and yet as soon as she had a free Saturday, she expected me to drop everything and do stuff with her.

'Later.' I shot out the door before she could ask me

any more questions. It's not that Mum and I don't get on at all, but she doesn't like Flynn – she's made it clear she thinks he is rude and aggressive – plus she has an annoying tendency to act as if I'm about nine years old.

I ran down the road, looking forward to meeting Flynn. He'd done an early shift at his car-wash place today so he was free to take his little sister, Caitlin, to some party at midday. She was going back to a friend's afterwards. His mum and older sister, Siobhan, were working all day. We were going to spend the afternoon on our own at Flynn's place.

There was nothing wrong with this, of course. But I knew if I'd told Mum she would have just made a fuss about how much time I spent with Flynn. She didn't seem to appreciate that we went to different schools and, when you factored in all Flynn's jobs and our homework, we had hardly any time to ourselves.

I reached the high street and strolled down to the post office. Flynn had said he was picking something up for his mum and that I should meet him and Caitlin there.

The queue for the counters was out the door when I arrived. I caught sight of Flynn immediately, about halfway down the line. I made my way past the other customers – mostly elderly men and women – to reach him. He saw me coming and smiled. His presence filled the room.

'Hi,' I said breathlessly.

'Hi.' Flynn pulled me close, fixing me with his eyes as he bent his face to mine.

A few months ago I would never have let anyone kiss me so publicly. Now I didn't care. I only cared about being with him. I closed my eyes and let myself fall into the kiss. Falling was what our whole relationship felt like right now. Falling in love. Falling into each other. Like we were flying, floating down through endless air. The rest of the world rushing by, all we needed in our arms.

An elderly lady in the queue behind us tutted to her friend.

'No shame, these kids,' she muttered.

I smiled as I carried on kissing Flynn.

'Oh don't go on, Vi,' her friend sighed. 'Why shouldn't they?'

I felt Flynn smiling back.

'Cashier number four, please,' boomed the electronic voice above our heads.

'Cashier number four, please,' mimicked a loud, giggling chorus of little girls' voices.

Caitlin. I'd forgotten she was even going to be here. I pulled away from Flynn and opened my eyes.

I saw Caitlin immediately. She was just around the corner, lounging against the far wall of the post office, her face, so like Flynn's, wreathed in cheeky smiles. Two little blonde girls stood on either side of her. All three of them were doubled up with laughter.

'Cashier number four, please,' they repeated in even sillier voices, collapsing into more giggles.

I looked round at Flynn. He rolled his eyes. 'They're driving me mad,' he said.

'You taking all of them to this party?' I asked, sliding my arm round his waist.

Flynn nodded, then leaned over the barrier that separated us and scowled at them. 'You guys are total pains in the butt. You know that?'

The two little blonde girls giggled shyly up at him.

I nudged him. 'Those two have such a crush on you,' I whispered.

Flynn shook his head. 'Doesn't mean they take any notice of what I say,' he said back.

I grinned at this new image of Flynn. Aggressive, hard-headed and terrifying – and floored by a couple of eight-year-olds.

'Hi, River.' Caitlin was smiling up at me.

'Hi,' I said. 'I like your top.'

Caitlin peered down at the pink T-shirt she was

wearing. 'Thanks. Are you coming to my first Holy Communion?'

I frowned. I dimly remembered Flynn's mum mentioning something about a first Holy Communion the very first time I'd met her last year. I'd had no idea what it was then and I had no better idea now.

'Sure,' I said. 'What is it? When is it?'

Caitlin's friends giggled again. Caitlin herself turned to Flynn. She put her hands on her hips. 'You promised you'd ask her,' she said in an outraged voice.

Flynn's face suddenly clouded over. 'You know I'm not going,' he said harshly. 'So there's no point.'

We'd reached the head of the queue. 'Cashier number five, please,' the electronic voice boomed.

Flynn stepped swiftly away from us and strode up to the counter. I looked down at Caitlin. Her face was sulky and cross, her lips pressed firmly together.

'What happens at this Communion thing?' I said.

Caitlin lowered her eyes. I suddenly realised she was trying not to cry.

'You get to wear a party dress and stuff,' said one of the friends, smoothing down her hair.

'And have a party after,' added the other, grinning.

Caitlin looked up. 'It's really about taking the bread and wine for the first time,' she said sullenly.

'Oh.' I felt none the wiser, but decided there was no point asking more questions. Clearly it didn't really matter what the whole thing was about. That wasn't what was important to Caitlin, anyway.

I took the girls to the door of the post office. Caitlin was very quiet as we stood there, waiting for Flynn.

After we'd dropped the three of them at their party we walked to the bus stop to go back to his. It was raining and Flynn – who owned no coat apart from a completely hideous jacket he refused to wear unless it was actually freezing and he knew no one would see him – was soaked.

We stood, kissing, at the bus stop. Flynn's shirt was damp under my hands. I pulled away, laughing. 'You're making me all wet,' I said.

He reached out for me again, grinning. 'I'll take it off as soon as we get home, okay? And then I'll take off yours and I'll dry you . . . mmmn . . . Now come here.'

'Hey, Flynn.' I thought back to our conversations earlier in the week.

'Mmmn, yeah?'

'You never told me what it was like being suspended?'

'That's in the past now, let's not talk about it, yeah?' He tried to kiss me again.

'Okay.' I hesitated. If he wouldn't talk about last Monday's exclusion, maybe he would open up about something that was going to happen in the future. 'Why can't we go to Caitlin's Communion thing?'

His eyes locked onto mine. 'You know.'

'No. I don't. I didn't know anything about it, remember?'

'Don't be mad about that.' Flynn sighed. 'Mum did ask me to ask you, but I'm against the whole thing, so—'

'But Caitlin was really upset when you said you weren't coming,' I persisted.

A bus drew up and we got on. I followed Flynn up the stairs. The bus was virtually empty. We sat towards the back. Flynn put his arm round my shoulder and leaned in to me.

'Why can't you go for Caitlin?' I said. 'For your mum?'

Flynn's eyes darkened. I knew from long experience this was the time to draw back. That he was just seconds away from losing his temper.

That I shouldn't push it anymore.

'I think you're being selfish,' I said.

Flynn slammed his hand down hard on the seat beside him.

'You don't freakin' know anything about it, Riv,' he said. 'The whole thing's wrong. What Caitlin's doing, it's like something kids are brainwashed into – I mean she just sees it as a big excuse for a party, but it's actually about becoming a Catholic – about joining in with everyone else taking Communion. And you know what Communion is? What the bread and wine are supposed to mean? Jesus's body and his blood. *That's* what you're actually supposed to be eating. It's freakin' cannibal, Riv. It's disgusting.'

My heart pounded. His face, his angry face, was terrifying.

I put my hand on his arm and took a deep breath. 'I don't see why any of that means you can't be there for Cait,' I said. 'I mean, how often does she see your dad?'

'*What?*' Flynn frowned in exasperation. 'She hardly ever sees him. Not since she was about three . . . you know, since . . .'

I nodded. Since their dad had attacked Flynn for trying to protect his mum and his mum had finally chucked him out of the house.

'I mean, obviously she's aware of him,' Flynn went on. 'Times he's come round to the flat drunk

34

– but she's got no money so he's not . . . what's that got to do with me going to her first Holy Communion anyway?'

I smiled. 'I'm just trying to make you see how important you are to her. I mean she hardly knows her dad. *He* won't be going to the first Holy Communion. You're the closest thing she's got to a proper father.'

Flynn stared at me.

'It's true,' I persisted. 'Look. It doesn't matter how you feel about what she's doing.'

'But . . .'

'Everyone knows you hate it,' I said firmly. 'But it's not about you. It's about Caitlin. She needs to know you're supporting her.'

I sat back and looked across the aisle and the empty seats on the other side of the bus, out through the opposite window. Rain glistened on the glass, lit up by the sun which was just emerging from behind a dark cloud.

After a minute I felt Flynn's hand on my arm.

I turned round.

'I hate you,' he said grumpily. But all the anger had gone from his face.

'Yeah?' I smiled at him. 'For being right?'

He stared at me for a second. 'Not exactly.' His eyes sparkled, more green now than gold in the sudden sunlight.

He leaned forwards, but I drew back, still smiling. 'Why then?'

Flynn sighed. He leaned towards me again, his eyes pulling me in.

'For being so freakin' perfect,' he whispered.

5

Flynn and I spent the afternoon at his flat, making out then doing homework in Flynn's tiny bedroom. It was ironic – considering what a rebel everyone thought Flynn was – that since I'd met him, I'd spent more time on my GCSEs than I ever did before. Flynn worked hard himself – determined to get the A levels to get to university to study for a law degree. In between drama research and French translation I tried to make Flynn talk about his school suspension again, but he kept changing the subject so I gave up.

Grace called towards the end of the afternoon. 'Hey, d'you two want to come over to James's tonight?' She sounded excited. 'His parents are going away for some last-minute anniversary thing and we've got the house to ourselves. *All night.*'

I hesitated. Spending the evening with Grace and James would be brilliant but there was no way

Mum would be happy about me staying away overnight with Flynn. Plus, Emmi was bound to be there, which meant Alex would be too – and last week's swimming pool fight was still fresh in my mind.

'I don't know,' I said.

'Oh, but Riv, it'll be awesome.' Grace sounded deflated.

'Let me talk to her.' That was Emmi in the background. A second later she was on the line. 'River, what's the problem?'

Flynn had stopped writing his essay and was watching me from across the room, his head tilted slightly to one side.

'Mum won't let me stay out all night.' I glanced at Flynn. 'And the last time your boyfriend saw my boyfriend out of school he nearly drowned him . . .'

Emmi lowered her voice. 'Alex and I won't be there, we're going to a concert. And Grace will be totally crushed if you don't come. She was really looking forward to it.'

I thought rapidly. If Emmi and Alex weren't going to be there, then only Mum stood in my way. Then another thought struck me. Emmi's parents were way more liberal than mine, but they had a big thing about concerts and festivals. From what I could gather, they appeared to believe that any hapless teenager turning up to watch live music was likely to be offered crack along with their hand stamp.

'What are you saying to your parents?'

Emmi sighed again. 'I don't know. I was hoping Louise would cover for me, but she's not around.'

Louise was Emmi's cool older sister, back at home after uni, and generally tolerant of Emmi's social life. Across the room Flynn was still watching me, his eyes raised.

'I've got an idea,' I said to Emmi. 'Why don't you tell your mum you're at mine? If you do that and I say I'm staying at yours we can spend the night wherever we want.'

'Awesome,' Emmi said.

I came off the phone. Flynn was frowning. 'You're going to lie to your mum?' He sounded worried. 'Are you sure, Riv?'

'She's not giving me a choice.' That was true, wasn't it? Mum totally hated Flynn. There was no way she would agree to us spending the night together. In fact, she would completely freak. Lying really was my only option.

Flynn said nothing.

I called Mum and told her I was going to stay over at Emmi's but that I was looking forward to coming back for lunch on Sunday with her. This last bit wasn't really true of course, but Mum seemed pleased. And Flynn's mum was delighted when she got home and he told her we were going to Caitlin's first Holy Communion.

'That's wonderful,' she said, her whole face lighting up. 'Thank you.'

'It's River you should thank,' Flynn said, shooting me one of his quick, rare smiles.

His mum squeezed my hand. 'Bless you, River, you've no idea how much it'll mean to Caitlin to have you both there.'

I shrugged, feeling embarrassed. 'I didn't say much,' I muttered. 'Not really.'

'He wouldn't be doing it for anyone else,' Flynn's mum said.

The day drifted lazily and happily into evening. I borrowed a change of clothes from Flynn's sister, then Flynn and I went over to James's house. I never ceased to be struck by the contrast between Flynn's Holloway Road flat with its cramped rooms and permanent smell of damp and James's detached mansion full of expensive furnishings and surrounded on all sides by a carefully manicured lawn. At least Flynn and James didn't ever seem bothered by the difference in their backgrounds.

Grace and James heated up some pasta and the four of us had a great time eating and chatting and watching movies on James's huge home cinema screen.

I sent Mum a text at ten-thirty to reassure her I was enjoying my fake evening at Emmi's. Then I switched off my phone. At about midnight, the four of us settled down in front of some cheesy horror film. After about half an hour it was obvious James and Grace were no longer actually watching the movie.

Flynn nudged me. 'D'you wanna see if we can find the room where we're sleeping?' he grinned. 'James said it was right at the top of the house.'

I nodded. He took my hand and led me towards the stairs. As we passed the study I blushed. At the last-night party after *Romeo and Juliet*, I had got Emmi to come on to Flynn in that very room. It had been a stupid test to see if he liked her better than me, something I'd been insecure about for months. I'd stopped Emmi before she'd gone all that far – but Flynn had been understandably furious when he'd realised what was happening.

Flynn glanced over and saw my cheeks reddening. 'Remembering your finest hour?' he said wryly.

The house was built over three floors. We went all the way up, to where a short corridor led away from the stairs. Flynn led me to the door on the right. It opened into a small guest room – plain cream walls, silky blue curtains at the window and a matching bedspread on the double bed. A small white-tiled shower room led off the bedroom, complete with fluffy towels and fresh toothbrushes.

'It's like a hotel room,' I gasped, delighted.

'James said you'd like it.'

We stared at each other for a minute.

Flynn put his hands on my waist and dipped his head down to mine. His eyes were soft gold in the little bedside light. 'Hey, River,' he breathed. 'I can't believe this is really happening.'

For a single, worrying moment I thought he was talking about us having sex. I'd made it clear to Flynn a few months back that I didn't feel ready yet. And just because we were spending the night together it didn't mean my feelings were any different now.

I looked away.

Flynn took my cheeks in his hands and turned my face back to his. 'I didn't mean *that*,' he said with a gentle smile.

I smiled back, grateful that he understood without me needing to talk about it. I wasn't sure what I was so apprehensive about. I just knew that losing my virginity was a massive step.

'What did you mean, then?' I raised my eyebrows

and grinned, trying to lighten up the conversation. 'That you're getting to sleep in a smart room for once – with a proper double bed?'

Flynn's eyes widened. 'Right. You're gonna die for that.' He pushed me onto the bed then leaped on top of me, tickling my ribs, down into my waist. I squealed and wriggled away from him until I was half lying off the bed. Flynn reached for me. I pushed him away with a massive shove that sent me toppling backwards off the bed. I hit the floor with a loud thump and lay there, winded.

'Riv?'

I kept my eyes tight shut. I could just picture Flynn's beautiful face above me on the bed, his fringe flopping down over his eyes.

'Riv, are you okay?'

It was almost impossible not to laugh. I kept my eyes very still, trying not to breathe.

'River?' I heard Flynn scrambling off the bed, felt his hand on my face. 'River?' His voice was suddenly terrified. Like a little kid's.

I opened my eyes and grinned up at him.

'What the . . . ?' His face was drawn. 'Oh, man, I thought . . . I thought . . .'

I stared at him. He looked completely panic-stricken, his breath coming out in ragged gasps. He sat back and covered his face with his hands. 'Don't freakin' *do* that, Riv.' His voice cracked. 'Please. Don't ever do that again.'

I scrabbled up onto my elbows. 'It was just a joke, Flynn. Why are you . . . ?'

'That's how my mum looked when we found her,' he whispered through his fingers. 'After Da hurt her. The time she went to hospital.'

6

Flynn was still kneeling beside me, his face in his hands. I reached out towards him, guilt flooding through me. 'I'm sorry,' I said. I touched his arm, wanting to pull his hands away from his face, to hold him, to make up. How could I have been such an idiot? 'I'm so, so sorry.'

Slowly Flynn let me pull his wrist away. He looked up. The terrified, vulnerable look had gone completely.

'Don't feel sorry for me,' he said. His voice sounded harsh, but I could hear the hurt underneath.

'I'm not,' I stammered. 'But it . . . must have been awful.'

Flynn shrugged. 'Just forget it.'

'But—'

'I made it up. It was a joke.'

What?

I stared at him, completely bewildered. 'How could you joke about *that*. About finding your *mum unconscious*.'

'Yeah well, I'm an excellent actor, remember?' Flynn gave another shrug.

For a second I felt so furious with him I wanted to scream. Then I caught the slight tremble of his mouth and I suddenly realised that he hadn't been joking at all. His reaction had been totally genuine and now he was pretending because he hated that I'd seen how upset he'd been.

'Stop making out it didn't affect you.' Tears leaked from my eyes. Why couldn't he just admit how hurt he had felt? Why was it always so hard to get him to open up? 'Whatever you say, it was a big deal, how your mum got beaten up, how your dad nearly . . .' I couldn't quite bring myself to say out loud just how close Flynn had come to being killed when his dad attacked him.

There was a heavy silence as I walked away and sat down on the end of the bed with my back to him.

I sat there for a long time, staring at the carpet. At last I felt the bed move as he sat down beside me.

'Making jokes is a way of dealing with it, Riv.'

I looked at him. 'Jeez, Flynn. I get that. But you *weren't* joking, were you?'

46

Another long pause. Flynn looked down at the silky blue bedcover between us.

'Siobhan found her first.' He stopped.

I glanced at him. He was still staring down at the bed. I sat quite still, waiting.

'I came into the room,' Flynn went on, his voice hollow, 'but Siobhan made me go out again. She said Mum was going to be okay. You see, it was Siobhan who saw our dad hit her and Siobhan who phoned for the ambulance. She was twelve. Too scared to tell the police what had happened. It changed her forever. Before then she was just a bit shy. Afterwards she became like . . . like this nervous wreck . . .'

I bit my lip. Flynn lay back on the bed.

'Sometimes I think that what my dad did to Siobhan was worse than what he did to me. You know, actually hurting me.' He put his hand on his forehead and stared up at the ceiling. 'I wish I'd been older. Stronger. I wish I'd realised sooner . . .'

I leaned back beside him and gazed at his profile – at the slope of his nose and the curve of his lip. 'You did what you could,' I said softly. 'You were only a kid.'

He turned and looked at me, his eyes unbearably sad.

'It wasn't enough,' he said. 'It just wasn't enough.'

I stroked his face, wishing I could take away the pain for him.

Knowing that I couldn't.

We fell asleep with our arms wrapped around each other. I had the sense of falling again, falling into him, losing any sense of where I ended and where he began. I woke once in the night and everything was still. Just the sound of our breathing and the wind in the trees outside.

I sighed. A deep, deep sigh, knowing that I would remember this moment for as long as I lived.

This perfect moment.

'River, Flynn, wake up. *Please.*'

I swam up towards Grace's voice through a deep sleep. Flynn and I were still lying where we'd fallen asleep, our arms wrapped around each other.

I opened my eyes. Flynn was frowning, blearily, towards the end of the bed. I followed his gaze.

Grace was standing just a metre away in one of James's old T-shirts, her hair tousled and her hands clasped anxiously together.

'James says you have to get up, Flynn. It's nine-thirty and he's worried you'll—'

'*What?*' Flynn sat bolt upright. 'I have to go right

now or I'll be late for Goldbar's.' He glared at Grace. 'Why didn't you wake us earlier?'

Grace's lip trembled.

'Hey.' I put my hand on Flynn's shoulder. 'It's not her fault.'

'Right.' Flynn scowled. 'Sorry.'

Grace nodded and scurried away.

Flynn blew out his breath, then leaped out of bed, scrabbling on the floor for his shoes. He pulled them on, then crept back onto the bed beside me.

He nuzzled my neck. 'I wish I could stay,' he murmured.

I ran my hand down his back. 'Can't you be late for work?'

He groaned. 'Don't tempt me.' He scooped me up, wrapping the sheets round me. 'I'll call you later. Okay?'

We lay there for a moment, just staring at each other.

'It was awesome being with you all night,' he said.

'The best.' I gazed up at him. 'This is the happiest I've ever been.'

'Say *what*, babe?' Flynn grinned – all cocky and happy. '*This* is just the *beginning*.'

He kissed me then pushed himself off the bed. I watched him lope away towards the door. He paused in the doorway, his hands on the door frame, as if he was going to turn round and say something.

I wanted to call him back. Back into bed. Back where I could run my hands down his smooth back and feel the muscles tensing under my fingers. I wanted to tell him how we couldn't make anything better. How I wanted to keep things exactly as they were right now. Perfect. Complete.

But I said nothing. And he walked away.

I had a shower in the sweet little bathroom, then got dressed and wandered downstairs. James made Grace and me some toast, then he drove us home in his brother's car.

He dropped me first, a couple of streets away from my house in case Mum saw us. I wandered dreamily home, my mind still focused on last night. As I turned my key in the door I reminded myself that I was supposed to have been at Emmi's all evening.

Mum's scream pierced through my head like a knife.

'Oh my goodness, River. Where have you been?' She rushed towards me like a whirlwind. Her face was all pale and her eyes strained and red. As she reached me, the relief on her face transformed into rage. 'Emmi's mum called here at one a.m., asking where Emmi was,' Mum shrieked. 'She thought Emmi was here. I thought you were with her. We've been up all night trying to find you.'

I stared at her, desperately trying to find a way of making out the whole thing had been a misunderstanding.

'We changed our minds about staying in,' I stammered. 'We went to another friend's house. It just got too late to call, so we crashed there, where . . .'

'Don't lie to me.' Mum's eyes were completely wild. She gripped my shoulders again. For a second I thought she was going to hit me. 'Emmi's mum called about an hour ago. Emmi was out all night too, that's why *she* didn't answer her phone either.' Mum sucked in her breath. Then she lowered her voice. 'You were with Flynn,' she said. 'Weren't you?'

I gulped.

'We just went to James's house . . .' I said. 'We didn't do anything wrong.'

Mum's eyes widened. 'Nothing wrong?' She gritted her teeth. 'What about lying to me yesterday? What about not answering your phone last night?'

My heart pounded. Of course, I'd switched off my mobile before we watched that stupid horror film. I'd been in such a daze this morning I hadn't even bothered to switch it back on yet. 'I'm sorry.' I couldn't see what else to say.

'Sorry?' Mum shook her head slowly. 'I don't know what's happened to you, River. I really don't. A few months ago you would never have dreamed of lying to me like that.' She paused and when she spoke again her voice was so ice cold that it sent a shiver down my spine. 'What has that boy done to you? Is he giving you drugs or something?'

'Mum.' The idea of Flynn – who I'd never even seen sip at a beer – pushing drugs at me was so ludicrous that I laughed.

Big mistake.

Mum grabbed my arm. Tight. 'And I suppose you spent the whole night in bed with him too?'

My face reddened. Mum was the last person I wanted to talk to about sex, so she had no idea I'd told Flynn that I wasn't ready yet.

'Well? you're too young for all of that.' Mum drew herself up. 'I don't want you seeing him again.'

'No.' I wrenched my arm away. 'You can't make me.'

'Oh yes I can,' Mum snapped. 'I'm going to talk to your father. I'm sure when he hears what a bad influence Flynn is, he—'

'Dad won't tell me not to see him,' I yelled. 'Dad's not a total Nazi. Unlike you.'

'Don't talk to me like that. Get upstairs to your room.'

I stared at her again. Mum hadn't tried to send me to my room since I was about twelve. I suddenly realised that what I'd said was true. There *was* no way she could make me do anything. Not anymore.

'No.' I spun round and pulled open the front door, my heart beating fast.

'Get back here.'

I stalked outside and onto the pavement. A sense of power surged through me. Now, *that* really was a drug. I strode towards the bus stop, high on my own invincibility, ignoring the yells that followed me down the street.

7

I slowed down as I approached Goldbar's, the boxing gym where Flynn worked on Sunday mornings in return for his boxing training. I'd never been there before, and I sensed that Flynn wouldn't be entirely happy about me just turning up. I found the place easily enough. A tatty, faded awning hung over the two high windows. I hesitated for a moment, reluctant to go inside. Still. Flynn would understand. This was an emergency.

The front door – a heavy, steel fire door – was open, so I slipped inside and walked down a short concrete corridor. It opened out into a small reception area. Very basic – just a wooden table and a couple of chairs in the corner. In the distance, through a doorway, I caught a glimpse of three big punchbags in a row.

I went up to the man at the table. He was reading a magazine which he didn't put down until I was standing right in front of him. We stared at each other for a few seconds. He was greasy-haired, with hooded eyes and a bored expression.

'Yeah?' His gaze flickered down my body, resting on my chest for several, very obvious, seconds.

I drew my jacket round me.

'I . . . er . . . is Flynn here?' I stammered.

The man looked up at my face, then jerked his thumb at the open doorway. He bent over his paper again.

I wandered across the corridor and through the door.

It was a large open room, smelly with that male stink of trainers and sweat. Two boxing rings, one of which was surrounded by people, were positioned beyond the row of punchbags. Otherwise the room was empty of furniture – just a pile of mats and a few plastic chairs stacked in one corner.

'Can I help you, love?' A big man standing on the other side of the door with his arms folded was staring at me. He didn't smile, but at least he wasn't looking at my chest.

'I'm looking for Flynn?' I said nervously.

The man unfolded his arms. I caught a glimpse of a long, snaking tattoo on the inside of his arm. He cupped his hands to his mouth.

'Flynn!' he yelled.

55

Everyone standing around the boxing ring turned round. I could feel my face reddening as they stared at me. They were all men. Most of them looked as if they were in their teens and twenties; a few were much older.

My eyes darted from one to the other, desperately looking for Flynn. Some of the men were laughing, nudging each other. Others were staring at me, like the guy outside had. Others still looked massively annoyed at the sight of me, presumably for distracting everyone. These were mostly the older guys. They turned quickly back to the ring. But both the boxers were hanging onto the ropes, grinning.

'You Flynn's bird?' one of them shouted.

I nodded, too embarrassed to speak.

'Flynn.' The boxer yelled in the direction of a door at the far end of the room. 'Get your arse out here.'

One of the older guys clapped his hands together. 'Come on. Get on with it,' he growled.

A few of the men turned back to the ring. But most of them – including the two boxers – were still staring at me.

Seconds later Flynn appeared at last. His eyes widened as he saw me.

'Couldn't ya wait till later, Flynn?'

'Go on, son.'

'She legal?'

He gritted his teeth against the shouts and laughs and catcalls from the guys beside the ring. Then he loped towards me, his normal swagger slightly exaggerated. He looked cross, which I knew meant he was embarrassed. So was I. In fact, I don't think I'd ever been more embarrassed in my life.

It seemed to take ages for him to travel the room. At last he was standing beside me. He grabbed my arm and took me – against a chorus of wolf whistles – out into the corridor.

'What are you doing here?' he hissed.

I gulped, tears pricking at my eyes. 'Mum found out I lied about last night,' I said. 'She threw me out.'

Yes, okay, I was exaggerating. But I sensed that Flynn wouldn't have much patience with a less dramatic explanation.

'What?' he frowned. 'Really?'

'Well,' I said, uncomfortably. 'She didn't exactly say I could never go back, but she told me I couldn't ever see you again.' A lump pressed against my throat. 'She said you were a bad influence.'

Flynn laughed. 'Silly cow,' he said, putting his arm round me. A tear trickled down my face. 'Hey, don't be upset. She can't do that.'

'No?' I looked up at him, sniffing.

He smiled. 'No. See, you're here with me right now, aren't you?'

'Oy, Flynn!' It was one of the older men who'd been annoyed before. 'Get laid on your own time!'

Flynn rolled his eyes. 'What a jerk,' he whispered, kissing my forehead. 'Whenever that guy's left in charge he—'

'Flynn, do you want to keep this job?'

Flynn clenched his jaw. 'I'll freakin' . . .'

'No. Go back.' I wiped my eyes. 'I'll be fine. I'll . . . I'll see you later.'

Flynn shook his head. He dug his hand in his pocket and drew out a couple of keys. 'Take these. Go to mine. Wait there. I'll be back in a couple of hours.'

He thrust the keys in my hand, kissed me again, then turned and headed back towards the boxing room. As he walked inside, I heard the guys from before break into catcalls and wolf whistles.

I wandered slowly up the Holloway Road towards Flynn's flat. My mind was whirling – Goldbar's was horrible. Far worse than I'd imagined. How could Flynn bear working there? And what was I going to do about Mum? It was all very well Flynn saying she couldn't prevent me seeing him. Maybe she couldn't. But there were all sorts of things she *could* do – like stop giving me any money or covering my mobile bills.

I trudged along the pavement to the entrance of Flynn's building. I let myself into the damp-smelling hallway and climbed the narrow stairs to the second floor. Flynn's flat was tiny: a little living area with a kitchen bar – not even a table and proper chairs – and only two small bedrooms, one which his mum and Siobhan shared and one with a curtain dividing the space into two, for him and Caitlin.

I opened the flat front door and headed for the living room. All of a sudden I heard voices. Laughing voices. They were coming from the room Siobhan shared with her mum. I froze. I hadn't expected anyone to be here.

'Siobhan?' It was a man's voice. Deep and cheerful. 'Okay, then. Tell me you don't.'

Another laugh. Nervous this time, and female – it must be Siobhan. I'd never heard her laugh before. And who was the man? Surely not Flynn's father. He sounded too young. Anyway, I couldn't imagine Siobhan laughing like that with her dad.

Silence.

My mouth was dry. I didn't know what to do. Part of me wanted to leave the flat, but I'd promised Flynn I'd wait here and I didn't have anywhere else to go. I knew that I should probably knock on Siobhan's bedroom door to let her know I was here, but that seemed far too embarrassing. The door to the kitchen-cum-living room was open in front of me. I went inside and perched on one of the large beanbags at the far end of the room.

Several long minutes ticked by. At last Siobhan and the man emerged into the narrow corridor.

'Okay then, beautiful.' The man sounded like he was smiling.

There was a slightly slurpy, sucking sound – like lips pulling apart. Then the front door opened and shut again. I could hear Siobhan humming as she walked back up the corridor. I sat on my beanbag watching the doorway. My heart raced. Any second she was going to see me. Any sec—

'Aaagh!' Siobhan clutched at the door frame as she screamed.

I jumped up. 'Sorry. Sorry. Flynn gave me the key and . . .'

'Oh my goodness.' Siobhan's green eyes were wide with shock. 'How long have you . . . ? Flynn's not here, is he? I thought he was at work?'

'He is,' I said. 'I'm sorry I frightened you. I . . . er . . .' I nodded towards the corridor behind her. 'I didn't know you were here with anyone.' I grinned. 'You kept that quiet.'

Siobhan's eyes sparkled as she blushed. 'There's nothing going on,' she said coyly.

I rolled my eyes. 'That's not what it sounded like from in here,' I said.

Siobhan slapped her hand over her mouth. 'You never heard us,' she squeaked.

I stared at her. I'd never seen her look so animated. So alive.

'A little,' I admitted. 'Enough to know he's massively into you.'

'D'you think?' She smiled excitedly at me. 'He's asked me out and I really like him, but . . .' She bit her lip. 'I don't know.'

I patted the beanbag beside me. 'Come and tell me,' I said.

Siobhan slid over and sat down. 'Promise you won't say anything?' she said.

'Who to?' I said. 'Your mum?'

Siobhan shook her head. I glanced down at her hands. *Jeez.* They were trembling. 'She knows. At least she knows Gary's asked me out. It's not her . . .' She looked down.

Of course. 'You don't want Flynn to know?' I said.

Siobhan shrugged nervously. 'He'll get mad. He'll worry Gary'll hurt me or something. You know how overprotective he gets, all that walking me home from the salon.'

I frowned. 'I thought you liked him doing that?'

'I did,' Siobhan admitted. 'But now . . .' She tailed off.

'Now there's Gary . . . ?'

Siobhan nodded.

'Tell me about him,' I said.

Siobhan hesitantly explained how Gary was a hair stylist – the son of the man who owned the salon where she worked. From what she said, he sounded not only lovely, but awesomely hot. For a moment, Siobhan's eyes lit up as she spoke, then she sighed. 'But I still don't know if I should go out with him.'

'Why? What's the problem?' I stared at her, bewildered.

Siobhan curled up on her beanbag. 'I'm scared,' she said. She looked at me. 'I mean, suppose he turns out to be like Da . . .' She paused, twisting her long, pale fingers together. 'Or Flynn?'

'Like Flynn?' I looked at Siobhan, a chill settling on my chest. 'Flynn would never hurt a girl. He's never hurt me.'

'Not physically, maybe,' Siobhan said. She kept her green eyes fixed on me. 'But he's scary when he's angry, isn't he?'

'He's just passionate,' I said defensively. 'People don't understand how strongly he feels about things.'

Siobhan looked away.

'Anyway, we were talking about you and Gary,' I said, eager to change the subject. 'Why not just give him a chance? Go to the cinema or out for a coffee with him? Something simple. You don't have to do anything you don't want.'

'You're right.' Siobhan nodded. 'It's just ... just such a big deal.' She looked up at me. 'Um, River, you promise you won't say anything to Flynn, will you?'

'No.' I knew I was making a mistake promising that. But what choice did I have? 'No. Course I won't.'

8

Flynn arrived home a couple of hours later. We talked for a bit about how ridiculous Mum was being, agreeing again that there was no way she could stop us seeing each other. I persuaded Flynn to come home with me so we could try and reason with Mum together. I had some vague hope that if I could just get Mum to have a proper conversation with Flynn then she would realise how great he really was.

I don't know what planet I was on.

Mum appeared in the hallway just as we shut the front door. She had obviously been crying. I felt a pang of guilt at the sight of her exhausted, tear-streaked face.

'So you've decided to come home, then?'

'Mum?' I said. 'I'm so sorr—'

'What's he doing here?' Mum shot a poisonous look at Flynn.

I put a restraining hand on Flynn's arm. 'He's come with me so we can talk to you,' I said quickly. 'I'm really sorry about last night, Mum. But it wasn't Flynn's fault. It wasn't his idea to do that switch thing with Emmi. That was—'

'I don't want to hear it,' she said. 'One lie after another. You have no idea what you're putting me through.'

I could feel Flynn's arm muscles tensing under my hand. I didn't dare look at his face. I could just imagine the thundercloud building behind his eyes.

'Please, Mum,' I said desperately. 'I don't want to—'

'I am so disgusted with you,' she shouted. 'You stupid little—'

'Don't speak to her like that.' Flynn's voice slammed down on Mum's like a sledgehammer.

She turned on him instantly.

'How dare you shout at me,' she yelled. 'Encouraging River to—'

'How dare *you* shout at *us*,' Flynn yelled back. 'We haven't done anything wrong. Nothing. You just can't accept . . .'

'Get out.' Mum pointed to the front door.

Flynn stood there, staring at her, his fists clenched.

My heart sank. Having promised me he would make every effort to keep his temper, Flynn had lost it completely in less than a minute. I looked at Mum again, at the way her lips were pressed meanly against each other. There was no way she was ever going to approve of Flynn. No way she was ever going to be happy about my seeing him.

'Mum?' It came out as a whisper.

She turned to me, her eyes hard and narrow. 'Obviously, I can't stop you going out with him, River. Not without locking you inside the house whenever you're not at school. But I don't want him here. And I want you to let me know exactly where you are from now on. I'm going to speak to your dad about it, as soon as I can get hold of him. Yes, and you're not getting an allowance anymore. Not until you've come to your senses.' She turned to Flynn with a final sneer. 'Maybe without River paying for you all the time, you'll lose interest. Emmi's mother told me you're well known for your ability to take from others.'

Flynn's jaw dropped open as Mum spun round and swept away from us into the kitchen. He took a step towards her, a low growl in his throat.

'No.' I grabbed his arm. 'There's no point.'

I threw an angry look at Mum, then tugged him outside. We stomped away down the path.

'Can you believe she said that?' Flynn shouted – his voice deep and loud above the fierce hiss of the wind. 'She more or less accused me of being a thief – just like they did at school.'

He yelled the whole way to the park, and was still mouthing off about it when I dragged him across the grass to the bench outside the little café where we'd met on our first date a few months ago.

'How dare your mum say all that,' he hissed as we sat down. 'She's got no idea.'

I shifted uneasily on the bench. It was one thing for me to criticise Mum. But, even though I thought Flynn was right, I didn't like him talking about her like that.

'She's just worried about me,' I said.

'Don't defend her,' Flynn said. 'She's punishing you for how you feel.'

'No, it's because I lied to her . . .'

'No way. She just doesn't like the fact that she can't control what you do anymore, so she's latching onto rumours she's heard about me instead of listening to what *you* say about me.' He paused. 'Stupid cow.'

'Stop it,' I said. 'How would you like it if I talked about your mum like that?'

'My mum *isn't* like that.' He stared at me, outraged. 'I can't believe you can even compare . . .'

'That's not the point,' I said, my voice rising along with my temper. 'The point is that you're only thinking about yourself. You're just like those horrible men at Goldbar's, only thinking about how something affects you. Not caring what it's like for me. Standing there, while those guys laughed at me. Just like with Mum when—'

'I didn't ask you to come to Goldbar's,' Flynn said. 'And it was *me* they were laughing at.'

'They were disgusting,' I said, wiping away the tears that pricked at my eyes.

'They're just guys, Riv,' Flynn said exasperatedly. 'They—'

'They were total idiots. Acting like they'd never seen a girl before. Have any of them even got girlfriends?'

'Of course,' Flynn frowned. 'Sure they do. They were just taking the mickey out of me. It's what it's like there. I—'

'Why d'you go there then?' My voice was coming out all broken up, the tears impossible to hold back any longer. 'Or is it where you really belong? With the other idiots?'

I spun on my heel and stormed off to the opposite corner of the park. I hugged my jacket around me. How could Flynn and I have been so close, inside that perfect moment, less than twenty-four hours ago? And now like this? I wandered among the trees for a few minutes. I was so cold and so miserable. I hated fighting with Flynn. I wasn't even sure what we were fighting about anymore.

The wind was whipping through the trees and my tears were freezing on my face as I wandered back to the bench where I'd left Flynn. He was still sitting there, two plastic cups of tea beside him on the bench. He looked up as I walked over.

I stared at the tea. 'How did you know I'd be back?'

He shrugged. 'I was going to drink yours if you didn't show up soon.' A small smile flickered across his face. 'Just cos we're going to argue, doesn't mean we have to freeze to death.'

I picked up one of the plastic cups. It felt warm in my cold hand. I sat down and leaned against him, all the fight seeping out of me. Flynn put his arm round me. We sat there for a while, just sipping at the tea.

'Why does nobody else see it?' I murmured.

'See what?' I could hear the smile in his voice as he kissed my hair.

I tilted my face up to his. 'How awesome what we have is,' I said.

'They're freakin' idiots,' Flynn said. His eyes were all soft, dark green like the leaves above his head. He stroked my cheek. 'I love you so much,' he whispered. 'I'm sorry I shouted. I know I was rude about your mum, she's just not giving me a chance. And you're right about Goldbar's. Those guys *are* stupid. Well, most of them. But that's just how guys are.' He leaned closer and the whole world shrank to his eyes.

We kissed, a long, sweet, healing kiss. Then we talked again, more carefully this time. Flynn spoke calmly about what Mum had said, acknowledging my point that she was trying to protect me.

'I know she makes all these assumptions about you,' I admitted in turn. 'She thought you made me lie to her about spending the night at Emmi's.'

'That's ironic, isn't it?' Flynn said with a sigh. 'I was actually *against* you lying.'

'I know.' I sighed too, leaning against his chest. It was good that Flynn and I were talking like this, but all it seemed to do was highlight the huge weight of prejudice we were up against.

It got dark and Flynn walked me to the end of my road. We agreed we'd meet after school on Tuesday. Two days away. It felt like a lifetime to live through.

Mum was very quiet when I got back. She didn't mention either our earlier argument or Flynn himself. She didn't repeat her demand that I never saw him again. In fact, we hardly spoke to each other – only about practical stuff: when she would be home late during the week and what she was

70

cooking for supper. I expected her at least to ground me – but she didn't even bother to do that, though she repeated her insistence that she was not giving me any money for the foreseeable future.

I went to bed that night feeling horribly lonely.

The next day it was almost a relief to get to school. Emmi was full of how dreadful it had been with her parents. She'd been grounded for a week. But it still seemed as if she was getting off more lightly than I was. Her parents liked Alex. And they didn't blame him because Emmi had sneaked off to that club. They were mostly just cross with her for not telling them where she was going. They hadn't said anything about never seeing her boyfriend again.

'Your mum has got a point,' Grace said to me timidly. 'I mean Flynn is very moody. Even James thinks so, and he's his best friend. I can understand why your mum thinks he might not be good for you.'

I stared at her. 'Is that what you think?'

'No. Of course not.' But she blushed in a way that made me suspect she really thought the opposite.

'It's not that, Riv,' Emmi said, coming to Grace's rescue. 'It's just you gotta ask yourself why wherever Flynn goes you get this long line of annoyed people. I mean, why's he always so angry about everything?'

I didn't know what to say to them. It was true. Flynn *was* angry a lot of the time. Certainly most of the time he was with other people. But on his own he could also be sweet and tender and vulnerable.

Why couldn't he be like that more often?

Why did life wind him up so much?

Why wasn't being with me enough to make him happy?

9

I saw Flynn that Tuesday, then again at the weekend. I was supposed to visit Dad and Gemma at the commune on Saturday – Dad moved there to 'get out of the rat race', as he put it, when he and Mum split up – but I didn't want to go. It wasn't that I thought Dad would rip into me like Mum had – Dad was too chilled for that. It was more the idea of being cooped up at the commune, with nothing to do but feed the hens and hoe the vegetable patch, while Flynn and my real life went on in London.

We talked for a bit on the phone and I told Dad about my row with Mum. As usual, he was understanding. Just gave me one of his cheesy sayings about liars only hurting themselves. And he was cool about me not coming up to the commune, too.

'Okay, love,' he just said. 'I'd come to see you

instead, but I can't get away right now. Gemma's not been well.'

Mum, naturally, rolled her eyes when I told her Dad had agreed to me not visiting the commune this weekend. Which just made me even more annoyed with her. Since the big bust-up we'd continued to maintain an uneasy truce in the house – no rows, but hardly speaking to each other either.

The weekend passed. School on Monday was a good day. We had double English, which I liked, then drama, which I loved – and no maths. Grace, Emmi and I ate our lunch outside in the crisp wintry sunshine. We talked about the teachers and music and shoes and didn't mention any of our boyfriends once. It was fun.

As I left school, I wasn't even thinking about Flynn but suddenly – as I turned the first corner – he was there in front of me.

'Hi, Riv,' he said, a huge smile wrinkling his eyes. 'Thought I'd surprise you.' He held out a small package.

'What's this?' I stared at his face – the eyes hard and shining, the cheeks flushed with pleasure. I loved that face.

'Take a look.'

I gently unfolded the tissue paper to find a delicate silver bracelet with a tiny heart dangling from the chain. 'Oh,' I said, overwhelmed by the feelings that welled up inside me. '*Oh* . . .'

Flynn looked concerned. 'What's the matter?'

'Nothing.' Tears filled my eyes. 'It's just so beautiful.'

'It's not much,' Flynn said with a shrug. 'But it is real silver. Riv, I know you don't care about money and possessions but it's exactly five months since the day we met and the last couple of weeks have been rubbish for you and I'm trying really hard to – what was it you said? – be more open, so this is to show that I mean it.'

I hurled myself into his arms. As we kissed, I felt all the tensions of my ongoing argument with Mum seeping away. So what if she didn't want me to be with Flynn? He loved me. And that was enough for me.

Our kiss became a hug. I opened my eyes. Across the road, Emmi and Grace had just walked into view. They were deep in conversation, looking down the road in the opposite direction from where we were standing.

'So you like the bracelet?' Flynn asked, standing back and peering anxiously at me.

'I love it,' I said. 'But how did you afford it?'

Flynn smiled. 'A few extra shifts, that's all. I had a free period just after lunch. I went out to buy it then. Came here as soon as the bell rang to give it to you.'

I nodded. Flynn looked pleased. 'Go on, ask me anything you want.' He put on a sllly voice. 'I have nothing to hide, babe.'

I gazed into his eyes, burning bright with love, and I thought how lucky I was.

'Okay,' I said, my mind running over the things we hadn't talked about in the past few weeks. 'You never told me how you felt about being suspended – or what happened afterwards, when you went back to school.'

'It was fine,' Flynn said. 'Surprisingly fine. I got a lot of work done and nobody said anything when I went into school the next day and it's all over now and I haven't been in a fight since.'

He tilted his head to one side and peered at me, his fringe flopping over one eye. 'How am I doing with the opening up thing?'

He looked so cute, his eyes all full of laughter, that all I wanted to do was kiss him again. 'I'm so—' I started.

'Hot.' Flynn leaned closer, brushing my lips with his. 'Unbelievably hot. You *are*.' He drew back and stared at me, right into me, full of wanting me. My heart started thumping. 'And I'm unbelievably lucky.'

'Oy!' a loud male voice shouted. I started back, my eyes springing open. Alex was beside us. He grabbed Flynn by the shoulder and swung him around.

'What have you done with it?' he raged.

Out of the corner of my eye, I could see Emmi and Grace rushing across the road towards us. Alex shoved Flynn backwards. Flynn looked totally shocked. He clearly had no idea what Alex was angry about.

'Hey!' I said. 'Stop it!'

'Alex!' Emmi rushed up, her eyes wide. 'What's going on?'

Alex said nothing. Just stood, glaring at Flynn.

'What's your problem?' Flynn demanded.

Grace grabbed my arm. 'I got a text from James a few minutes ago. He said Alex was mad.'

'I can see that,' I said, 'but why?'

Alex pushed Flynn in the chest again. This time Flynn grabbed Alex's school blazer and pushed him back. They were seconds away from a full-on fight.

Emmi and I looked desperately at each other.

'Stop it!' I shouted at them both.

'Alex, what's the matter?' Emmi pleaded.

Alex took a deep breath. 'He stole my iPad.'

There was a terrible silence.

'*What?*' Flynn's lip curled with contempt. 'No I didn't.'

'Yes you did.' Alex was so angry he was shaking. 'I had it this morning, at school. When I went to my locker at the end of the day it was gone. You rushed out when the bell rang. It was you. It had to be. *You* took it.'

'No I freakin' didn't,' Flynn said. 'I was rushing cos I was coming here to see River.'

'I bet it's in your bag right now.' Alex lunged for the bag slung from Flynn's shoulder, but Flynn was too quick. He skipped backwards and Alex stumbled, arms outstretched. He turned on Flynn again, furious.

'Show me!'

'No freakin' way!'

'Flynn,' I said. *For goodness sake.* 'Why don't you just show him what's in your bag.'

Flynn threw me a furious glance. I was dimly aware of Emmi beside me, and Grace on Alex's other side, but I kept my focus on Flynn.

'You didn't take the iPad,' I said calmly. 'Showing him your bag will prove it.'

Flynn made a sound that was somewhere between a grunt and a growl. Angrily, he swung the bag off his shoulder and opened it up.

'There,' he said, shoving it at Alex. 'Go on, look.'

Alex snatched the bag and rummaged through it. He looked up, his eyes still livid. 'Okay, so it's not here. That just means you've already stashed it somewhere.'

'No,' I said quickly before Flynn could respond. 'Flynn came straight here. He wouldn't have had time.'

'Baby,' Emmi said, twisting her arm through Alex's. 'It does seem like you're jumping to conclusions a bit. I mean, why blame Flynn?'

I threw her a grateful glance.

Alex wrested his arm away from her. 'Because it's *got* to be him,' he said. 'It's just like with Nikki's purse the other day.'

'Rubbish,' Flynn said. 'I didn't take anyone's purse.'

'Are you calling me a liar?' Alex drew himself up.

'Stop it,' I said, taking Flynn's arm. 'Come on, let's go,' I threw Grace and Emmi a despairing look.

'Yeah, come on.' Emmi gripped Alex by the elbow and, much to my relief, steered him away.

Flynn let me lead him along the street in the opposite direction. Neither of us spoke for a few minutes. Now we were away from Alex, I couldn't stop thinking about the silver bracelet Flynn had bought me. Flynn never had any money. He'd never given me anything before. Was it really a coincidence that he should be accused of a theft on the very day he'd bought me a relatively expensive present?

'River?'

I looked up. Flynn glanced sideways at me. His expression was far more vulnerable than before.

'I didn't take the iPad,' he said miserably.

I stopped and took his face in my hands. 'I know.' But inside I wasn't sure. Flynn had said he'd done a few extra shifts to pay for the bracelet, but was that really true? He could have taken the iPad from Alex's locker this morning, then sold it and used the money – or some of it – to buy my bracelet during his free period from school.

Flynn pulled me to him in a hug, burying his face in my hair. 'Thank you for believing me.' His voice cracked. 'I think you're the only one. I . . . I don't know what I'd do without you.'

'Of course I believe you,' I said, hugging him back. I pushed my doubts away. What was I thinking? Flynn was no thief.

'I love you, River.'

I breathed in his words. This was exactly what I'd wanted. At last, Flynn was really opening up. A minute later we reached the end of my road. Flynn had work in half an hour – his organic vegetable delivery job – so we kissed, a long, lingering, beautiful kiss, and said goodbye.

I drifted home in a dream. And yet, happy though I was, shards of doubt still pricked at me. Could Flynn have stolen from Alex? If he had, it would hurt even worse than him getting provoked into fights where at least I could understand his anger. But stealing was a cold-blooded thing to do. Which – now I thought about it – surely meant Flynn *couldn't* be responsible. He was *never* cold-blooded.

Neither was I. In fact, if I was honest, the intensity of my feelings scared me. Whether Flynn was getting into fights or telling me he loved me, he dominated everything in my life. Nothing seemed real apart from being with him.

10

I met Flynn again the next day after school. We
hung out in the park, then I went with him to the
hair salon to pick up Siobhan. It had just gone six,
but Siobhan was still washing a woman's hair. She
signalled she'd just be a couple of minutes, so Flynn
and I sat down by the door. Flynn chatted to the
receptionist while I looked round, wondering
which of the two male stylists was the guy who'd
been with Siobhan the other day, Gary. One of the
men was short and stocky with spiky blond hair.
The other was tall and black with broad shoulders.

Flynn nudged me. 'Just going for a pee.'

He wandered off to the back of the salon and the
stairs down to the staff area.

I watched Siobhan expertly rinsing off her client's
hair. Her own red hair was tied neatly off her face.
She looked up, caught sight of Flynn disappearing

into the staff area, then smiled over at me. I smiled back.

Siobhan's eyes flickered over to my left, to the salon front door. Her eyes widened. The smile slid off her face.

I looked around. A tall, middle-aged man stood in the doorway. He was wearing a cheap grey suit that was too long in the sleeves and very worn around the collar. I frowned. There was something familiar about him – about the slope of his nose, the curve of his lip. But his face was fleshy and his skin red and shiny.

I looked back at Siobhan. She looked terrified.

Some instinct told me it had to be her and Flynn's dad.

I watched, open-mouthed, as the showerhead in Siobhan's hand drifted forwards. Water sprayed over the client's face. Siobhan didn't notice. She was still staring at the man in the doorway.

The client spluttered and sat up with a shriek.

Siobhan dropped the shower head in the sink and stepped backwards. Water was now spraying all over the floor. The client was still shrieking. All the other clients and stylists were looking around, bemused.

Siobhan covered her mouth with her hands. Even at this distance I could see her whole body was shaking.

I jumped up and turned towards the man. He was just inside the salon now. As I moved, his gaze shifted from Siobhan to me.

He smiled at me. And there was so much of Flynn in that smile that any remaining doubts I had about the man's identity disappeared.

'I'm Patrick Hayes,' he said, holding out his hand and completely ignoring the chaos going on in the salon behind us.

I shook it, my heart pounding. This was Flynn's da. The man who had beat his mum. Who had terrorised Siobhan. Who had left Flynn with a long scar across his shoulder.

'You're the girl Patrick is going out with.' He looked around. 'Patrick not here, then?'

Patrick. Flynn's first name. The one he refused to answer to because it was his da's name.

I stared at the man, unable to speak.

'It's nice to meet you,' he smiled. 'I've seen you out with Patrick before. He's got good taste.'

I swallowed. I'd expected a monster, but the man in front of me looked pretty normal. Charming, even. Okay, so his face was flushed and there was something clouded about his eyes, but he certainly didn't seem drunk. And his whole demeanour was humble. He was almost shuffling as he spoke to me, as if he were slightly ashamed of something.

I looked at his hands. They were shaking slightly. I was dimly aware of people talking rapidly across the room, though the client Siobhan had sprayed with water had stopped shrieking.

I opened my mouth, but still no sounds came out.

'I daresay you've heard about me?' Flynn's da said.

I nodded. He glanced towards the sinks. I followed his gaze. Most of the stylists were crowded around the sopping client, who was wiping her face with a towel. Someone was mopping the floor. Siobhan had shrunk against the far wall of the salon. She was still shaking. The black guy I'd noticed before was standing beside her, his hand on her shoulder.

'I was hoping for a word with Siobhan,' Flynn's da said.

I blinked at him. 'Now?' I stammered.

'Well . . .' Flynn's da looked towards the back of the salon. A look of alarm crossed his face. I followed his gaze. Flynn was there, in the doorway leading from the staff area. He was staring at the scene by the basins, at Siobhan in the corner. She was rushing towards him, pointing at the door.

I turned back. Flynn's da had gone.

Suddenly my legs felt wobbly. I sat down hard on the seat by the door.

Seconds later Flynn was at my side, his hand gripping my elbow. 'Are you okay, River? Are you all right?'

'Yes.'

Flynn raced to the door and peered along the street. Then he darted back to me and sat down, wrapping his arms around me. 'Oh, my . . . Are you . . . ? What did he do?'

I looked up at him. 'I'm fine. He didn't do anything. I . . .'

'Oh man, I don't believe it.' Flynn hugged me so tightly I could hardly breathe. 'I can't believe he was here. That he talked to you.' He rocked me in his arms, then sat back and held my face in his hands. His eyes blazed. 'Tell me what happened.'

As I spoke, Siobhan came over and sat down beside me, on my other side. She was still shaking.

Both she and Flynn were acting as if I'd gone through some terrible ordeal. I tried to reassure them.

'I'm fine,' I said. 'Honestly. He wasn't even drunk. At least, I don't think so. He said he just wanted to talk to Siobhan.'

Flynn and Siobhan exchanged glances. 'D'you think he knows about Sunday?' Siobhan said.

Flynn gritted his teeth. 'We'll have to cancel it.'

'We can't,' Siobhan said. 'Caitlin had to miss her

original First Communion because she was ill last June. If she doesn't do it on Sunday, she'll have to wait until after Easter. She'll be devastated.'

'I don't think he was going to make any trouble,' I said. 'I mean, look how he left without any fuss.'

Flynn pulled me closer towards him again. 'Oh, man . . .' His voice tensed with anger. 'If he'd hurt you. If . . .'

'He didn't, Flynn.' I squeezed his hand. 'He was fine. Really. Nice, actually. He said he'd seen me with you. Thought you had good taste.'

I was trying to make Flynn smile, but instead his face twisted with fury. 'He's seen us together? Freakin' hell, Riv, he's been watching us. I bet he'll come after you now.' He thumped the seat beside him so hard that it jumped.

I frowned. 'Flynn, you're not listening. He didn't *want* anything. Just to talk to Siobhan . . .'

'And what d'you think he wanted from her?' Flynn said. '*Money*. That's what. Freakin' money for a freakin' pint.'

I opened my mouth to try and explain again, but Siobhan put her hand on my arm. She shook her head, then indicated the salon behind her. Everyone was watching us.

'We should go,' she murmured. 'You take River

home, Flynn. Gary said he'd drive me back in his car.'

Flynn looked suspiciously into the salon. The black guy was gazing over at us. So that was Gary.

'He's sound,' Siobhan said. She glanced at me briefly. 'Go on, both of you.'

Flynn was clearly not completely convinced. I looked up at Siobhan and nodded. 'Come on, Flynn.' I smiled at him. 'Siob'll get home quicker this way.'

Flynn nodded. 'I guess.' He stood up and took my hand. 'You sure, Siob?' he said.

'Gary's really okay. Honest,' she said. 'He'll make sure I'm safe. He's already explained everything to his dad so he's not cross about the mess I made *and* he calmed down the client.'

This seemed to convince Flynn at last.

Siobhan went back to Gary, and Flynn and I wandered up the road. Flynn kept glancing around, his arm across my shoulder. I knew he was looking out for his da, but we saw no one all the way home.

We stood on the corner, kissing, for ages. Flynn's kisses were always like a conversation, where he listened to how I wanted to be kissed and told me how he felt. Today it was as if he was telling me over and over how much he loved me.

At last Flynn let me go. His eyes shone liquid gold in the street lights. 'Please be careful,' he whispered.

'Please, if my da ever comes up to you again, just walk away. Promise me?'

'I promise,' I said, kissing him again. 'I promise.'

At last he pulled away. I watched him stroll along the street, then I went inside and up to my room. Mum knocked to say she was going out and there was some food in the fridge.

I called out a plaintive thank you. Now I was on my own I felt kind of weird about having met Flynn's da and how much it had freaked out Flynn and his sister. I half hoped Mum would come into my room so we could talk like we used to.

But she didn't.

11

It was a long week. I missed Flynn and he missed me, but we both had school and Flynn had his jobs so I didn't see much of him until the following Friday. We couldn't even talk for long. Flynn never had much credit on his phone – for ages he hadn't owned a phone at all – and now, thanks to Mum cutting back my allowance, I didn't either.

Anyway I didn't want to speak to him on the phone. I wanted to see him. I wanted him to leave his jobs, to stop meeting Siobhan from work, to forget about his da and his homework and all his responsibilities.

I hated not having any money of my own. Flynn gave most of what he earned to his mum, so between us we had barely enough to scrape together the price of a cup of coffee. It made going out anywhere almost impossible. I'd already decided to get a job – which I suspected was going to mean another argument with Mum, who was bound to complain it would get in the way of my schoolwork.

By Thursday I was feeling really miserable. I thought I was covering it up quite well, paying attention in class and chatting to my friends, but as I wandered outside at break with Grace and Emmi, Emmi said, 'Okay, River, we've waited and waited and we're not waiting any longer. What on earth is wrong?'

I hadn't talked to either of them properly for a long time, especially about Flynn. In fact, I'd hardly seen them outside school. Not since the big bust-up with Mum, when they'd both made it clear they had mixed feelings about Flynn themselves.

I stood there, feeling the cold wind against my face.

'Come on, Riv,' Grace said gently. 'You haven't talked to us for ages.' She paused. 'Is it Flynn?'

'Not exactly . . . though . . . it's just I hardly ever see him,' I said.

Emmi raised her eyebrows. 'Some might count that a blessing,' she said drily.

'Fine,' I snapped. 'If you're just going to take the—'

'No.' Grace put her hand on my arm. 'Course we're not.' She frowned at Emmi.

'Sorry.' Emmi rolled her eyes. 'So, you miss him?'

I sighed. 'I do. And nobody else ever seems to understand why – or why Flynn sometimes acts a bit . . . passionate. It's not fair . . .' I hesitated. No one outside Flynn's family knew about his da or the true background to his anger and I didn't feel I could reveal any of it without Flynn's permission. 'It's just no one understands him,' I finished lamely.

'Come on, Riv,' Emmi said. 'Flynn doesn't exactly make it easy, does he?'

'You've got to admit he likes keeping people at a distance.' Grace made a face. 'Sometimes I think he *wants* people to be scared of him.'

I considered this. Maybe Grace was right. The wind whipped my hair across my face. As I brushed it back Emmi shook her head at me.

'You can't let him tell you what to do, girl,' she said slowly. 'I'd never let Alex boss me about.'

'He doesn't tell me what to do,' I said, immediately feeling disloyal that I'd talked about Flynn in the first place. 'I know he sometimes comes across as a bit defensive, but it doesn't help that everyone blames him whenever something goes missing.'

Emmi and Grace exchanged another look. I suddenly remembered my little silver heart bracelet and how it had appeared the very day Alex's iPad was stolen. Did they think Flynn was capable of that theft? Did I?

I quickly changed the subject to our weekend plans. Before I knew where I was I'd agreed to go to a party with the girls and James and Alex on Saturday night. I knew Flynn would be annoyed at having to socialise with Alex, but Grace said she was sure we could stay over at James's house again. I hoped that the memory of our fantastic night there would persuade Flynn that we'd have a good time.

It did. Sort of.

Even so, when we met up on Saturday after he'd done an early shift at the café, I could see he was in a bad mood. He sulked all the way through the party, refusing to talk to anyone except me and James. He was superficially polite to Grace, though I suspected that was simply out of respect for James. He ignored Alex and Emmi point blank, though neither of them seemed that bothered.

I felt exasperated with him. After defending him earlier in the week to Emmi and Grace, it was deeply annoying that he should act in exactly the way they'd described.

He was still in a bad mood when we got back to James's house. But then, as soon as we were on our own in the little room with the blue silky curtains he was so sweet. He lay me down on the bed and held me and stroked my hair. I felt like texting Emmi to tell her. But of course I didn't. Instead we talked. Flynn told me how much he'd missed me all week, how much he worried about me being safe. He also talked about Siobhan, how he worried about her – how nervy she'd been after their da's visit.

I felt like I should tell him about Gary, but it wasn't really my business and Siobhan had asked me not to. Anyway, I didn't want to bring up anything that would change the soft, loving mood he was in.

I texted Mum to say I wasn't coming home, that I was staying over 'with friends'. She wouldn't like it, of course, but then she didn't like anything I did at the moment as far as I could see. As soon as I'd sent the message I switched off my phone.

Flynn and I talked for hours, then woke up late the next morning. We had to rush to get back to his flat to be ready for Caitlin's first Holy Communion service. As we opened the front door to the flat the bathroom door just in front of us opened. Gary stepped out into the hallway.

I gasped.

Flynn jumped forwards and grabbed Gary's arm.

'What the—?' Before Gary even had time to register what was happening, Flynn slammed him against the wall. He rammed his elbow under Gary's chin.

'What are you doing here?' he hissed.

'Relax, mate. I've just come to meet Siobhan.' Gary frowned, pushing Flynn away with what I noticed were extremely muscular arms.

My breath caught in my throat. 'Flynn.'

Flynn pushed back, pressing Gary harder against the wall. 'You think taking her home once means . . . ?'

'Stop it.' Siobhan rushed into the hallway. 'It's okay. Flynn. It's okay.'

Flynn stared round at her. 'It's not okay,' he snapped.

His mum and Caitlin appeared in the living area door.

'Hey, come on, mate.' Gary's voice was tense, but still conciliatory. He was at least half a head taller than Flynn and broader too.

Siobhan glared at Flynn – angrier than I'd ever seen her. 'I said, stop it.'

My heart pounded. 'Please, Flynn.' I touched his arm. 'You're overreacting.'

He shot a look at me. 'Overreacting?' He blinked, his eyes searching my face. 'You *knew* . . . ?' He looked at Gary. 'Him and . . .'

'Me and Siobhan,' Gary nodded – still amazingly calm in the face of Flynn's anger. 'We're together.'

Flynn let go of him and staggered backwards. He looked at Siobhan. 'No.'

'Yes.' She put her hands on her hips. 'Now back off.'

Flynn looked from her, to his mum and Caitlin, then back to me.

'You *knew*?' he hissed.

I gulped. 'They were here that day you gave me your keys . . . when . . .'

'That was weeks ago,' Flynn yelled. 'How *dare* you not tell me what was going on?'

'Flynn, please . . .' My heart was in my mouth. His face was purple with rage. My hands started shaking.

'Listen, mate,' Gary said urgently. 'I get where you're coming from. If she was my sister, after what she's been through . . . I'd be the same. But you can't be there for her like I can. You can't . . .'

'I *can*,' Flynn yelled. 'She doesn't need you. She—'

'That's enough.' Siobhan gripped Flynn's arm and swung him round to face her. Her face was tight with fury. 'This is none of your business.'

Flynn frowned. 'None of my . . . ?' He turned on me again. 'Why didn't you tell me?'

I stared at him helplessly.

'Because I asked her not to,' Siobhan shouted. 'Because I knew how you'd react. For goodness sake, can you not see yourself?'

Flynn slammed the wall with his palm.

I jumped, so scared I felt sick.

'Don't tell me I'm out of order here. You're the one who's not been honest. And *you* . . .' He turned on me again.

'Please, Flynn.' I could feel the tears welling up again.

'Fine.' He threw his hands into the air and spun round. Then he stormed out, slamming the flat door behind him.

I burst into tears.

Siobhan put her arm round me and led me into her bedroom. I caught a quick glimpse of Flynn's mum and Caitin, both wide-eyed. Then Siobhan shut the door and sat me down on the bed. She perched beside me and stroked my shoulder.

'He's an eejit, my brother, sometimes. Honestly. I thought if he met Gary here, like it was a done deal, then he'd just accept it.'

I sniffed back my tears. Though I knew Flynn had overreacted, I did still feel guilty about not telling him about Gary.

'He just wants to protect you,' I said, wiping my eyes.

Siobhan stared at me, her expression all solemn. 'Goodness but you're loyal.' She hugged me. 'I know he does.' She sighed. 'Trouble is sometimes he over-does it. Overdoes everything. Like Da.'

I shifted round on the bed. 'Your dad?'

Siobhan nodded. 'Yeah. Flynn's so like him, you know. It scares me a bit. The way he loses his temper so quick.' She paused. 'That's like Da.'

I looked at her, at the concern in her green eyes.

My heart sank. Even his own sister thought he was too angry, too easily wound up, too out of control. 'Flynn's not always like that,' I insisted. 'Yeah he loses it sometimes, but he's funny and sweet and he . . . he . . .'

'He loves you.' Siobhan sighed. 'Yeah. I know he does. I've never seen him behave like he does around you. But still . . .'

A soft rap on the door. Gary poked his head round. 'Sorry to interrupt,' he smiled. 'Your mum says we need to be going.'

Siobhan looked at me. 'You all right?'

I nodded, wiping my eyes, then followed her out to the corridor.

12

Flynn's mum took my arm as we left the flat. 'So what d'you know about first Holy Communion, River?' she said.

'Not much,' I smiled weakly. I couldn't stop thinking about Flynn. Where had he gone? What was he doing? How could I make him understand why I'd had to keep my promise not to tell him about Siobhan and Gary?

Caitlin skipped past us in her long white dress, a sparkling tiara in her hands.

'She looks like she's getting married,' I said.

'Well, in a way she is.' Flynn's mum squeezed my arm. 'This is the moment where she commits herself to being a Catholic. To becoming part of the body of Christ. It's like a marriage, but to God.'

'Oh.' I didn't understand and I didn't know what to say.

'Taking Communion.' Flynn's mum smiled.

'Coming together. Sharing in God's love. Knowing that you're not on your own.'

We walked out onto Holloway Road. Flynn was leaning against the nearest lamp post, his arms folded. He stared grimly at us. At me. My eyes filled with tears again. All I wanted was for him to come over, to put his arms round me.

'Did Flynn do it?' I asked. 'Take Communion?'

'Oh yes,' his mum said softly. 'And it's still there, inside him, no matter what he thinks now.'

She turned away to answer some question of Caitlin's. I watched as Gary strolled over to Flynn. Siobhan fluttered about behind him, nervously twisting her scarf round her hand. Gary said something I couldn't hear. Flynn nodded, sullenly, then went up to Siobhan. They talked briefly. Siobhan pointed to me.

And then he was striding over. Right next to me. It was like the first time he ever spoke to me. His presence was overpowering. He shoved his hands in his pockets.

'Still here, then?' His eyes were fierce. Hurt.

I stared at him, feeling guilty. Should I have told him about Gary before? No. Siobhan had already told him she'd made me swear not to say anything. What did he expect me to do? Break a promise? My guilt morphed into resentment. It wasn't fair of him to make such a massive deal out of it.

Flynn's eyes softened. 'I'm sorry I got angry,' he said quietly. 'I was just worried about Siobhan.'

I nodded. Flynn reached for my hand. 'Like you said,' he muttered. 'Today is about Cait. Right?'

I nodded again and we walked on, to the church. I still felt troubled. Okay, so Flynn had apologised, but his whole body radiated repressed fury. He said very little as we strolled along, though he didn't let go of my hand. I couldn't work out exactly what was wrong. It was obvious he'd said sorry to Gary and to his sister, just as he had to me. But he was still tense, still angry, still full of his dark mood.

I walked with him into the church. It was small, with a table set with candles at the far end – that was the altar – and rows of seats on either side of a central aisle. Hardly anyone was sitting down yet, but the church was full of people milling around and chatting to each other. Flynn's mum made the sign of the cross over her chest, bowed to the altar, then disappeared somewhere with Caitlin. The rest of us walked up the side aisle. Siobhan pointed to a pew near the front. I was closest so I walked in, down to the central aisle. Flynn followed me, with Siobhan and Gary after him.

I glanced around the church. I'd hardly ever been inside one before. There was a statue of Mary in a blue dress holding baby Jesus at the front of the seats. Mary looked sad, I thought. Why was that?

After a few minutes some organ music started and everyone sat down. Flynn's mum appeared and I shuffled up to let her into the seat closest to the central aisle.

'There's only a few from the area making their first Holy Communion today,' she said distractedly. 'Still at least Caitlin's got a couple of friends with her.'

On my other side, Flynn was staring gloomily down at the floor between his feet. I craned my neck, wondering where Caitlin had gone. The church was almost full now, the last few people scuttling to their places. Organ music started and a procession began on the far side of the church. It was led by a man I assumed must be the priest. He was wearing full-length robes and carrying a large cross. More men in robes followed behind him, then three pairs of children. The little boys were in smart clothes, some even wore jackets. The girls were all wearing white dresses. I spotted Caitlin second in line. Her little face was screwed up with concentration as she measured out her footsteps carefully.

The procession turned at the foot of the seats and made its way up the central aisle. I smiled at Caitlin as she passed. She'd clearly got the hang of the pacing as her eyes were darting about, her face wreathed in a mischievous smile.

The service took about fifty minutes. During the actual Communion bit, Caitlin and her mum went up to the altar and took a wafer and a sip from the big goblet in the priest's hands. Then most of the church did the same. As Siobhan and Gary went up to the front, I glanced at Flynn. He was sitting firmly in his seat, his eyes still on the ground in front of him.

I wanted to say something, but I had no idea what would rouse him from his dark mood. I turned away and focused on the people shuffling sideways along the altar. I watched as the priest made the sign of the cross over each one. It seemed to take a long time, but at last everyone was sitting down again. I caught a whiff of alcohol as Siobhan passed me – so it was real booze then, in that shiny goblet.

Caitlin was now sitting between me and her mum. She wriggled now and then but, on the whole, kept very still as the priest started chanting in a low monotone, pausing to allow the congregation to make responses. I was just wondering how much longer it was all going to carry on – there was an order of service, but I hadn't been following it – when the door at the back of the church slammed. I turned, along with everyone else, to see who or what was there.

I blinked. Flynn's da was lurching up the central aisle, looking around. As I watched, his eyes fixed on Caitlin and he smiled. Flynn's mum gasped.

A split second later, Flynn's da reached us.

'My little angel,' he slurred, his hand clawing in Caitlin's direction.

Caitlin flinched, her eyes wide and scared. Her da stumbled sideways, still reaching out. Some protective instinct kicked in. I put my arm across Caitlin's body. Flynn's da scowled and grabbed my arm, trying to push me away.

'No,' I said.

In an instant Flynn was there, squeezing past me, forcing his da's hand off my shoulder.

'Don't touch her,' he hissed. 'Not her. Not them.' He shoved his da in the chest. His da stumbled, nearly losing his footing. 'Not them, you bastard.'

'Will you calm down, Patrick,' his da slurred, reeling. He staggered back a few steps, almost to the rear of the church. 'I'm just . . .'

'Don't call me that.' Flynn shoved his da again. But this time his da was tensed up, ready for the blow.

I looked around quickly. Everyone in the church was staring, wide-eyed, at what was going on.

'Stop it, son.' Flynn's da's voice rose angrily. He put out his arms to push Flynn away.

'Don't freakin' call me son,' Flynn shouted. 'I'm not anything to you. You're not anything to me.' And then he punched him. Smack. Right in his face.

With a roar his da swung a punch back. Flynn ducked. The arm sailed over his head. Flynn darted up. He moved in close. His fist rammed into his da's face again. 'You're nothing,' he shouted. He punched again. 'Nothing.' His da stumbled backwards. Again. 'Nothing.'

His da went flying to the ground.

People around me were yelling. I could hear Caitlin scream. I froze where I stood, horrified, as Flynn leaped down on top of his da. I caught a glimpse of his face, contorted with rage. And suddenly he was all fists. Slamming into his da's face. His da was pushing and punching at him too. Both of them yelling their heads off.

Men rushed past me. Gary was one of them. Siobhan ran after him, shrieking, followed by the priest and the other men in the long robes.

I could no longer see Flynn. Beside me, Caitlin was sobbing, clinging to her mum. Other little children were crying too. Everyone was talking.

Shouting. And over it all I could hear Flynn's roar; it barely sounded human.

I darted into the aisle, pushing my way to the back of the church. I didn't waste my energy on words, I yanked at people's arms, at their sides, clawing my way with nails and elbows to the front of the crowd.

I arrived just as Gary and some other guy were dragging Flynn off his da. They each had an arm, but Flynn was still kicking and screaming like a wild animal.

'You're not doing this anymore,' he yelled, almost hoarse. 'I'm not letting you.'

I caught a glimpse of his da's face, covered with blood. *Ugh.* I retched. Two more men had got hold of Flynn's legs now. It was taking four of them and they could still barely hold him back.

The noise was indescribable. All the men were bellowing at Flynn to calm down. Siobhan was next to him, shouting at him to stop, her face completely screwed up with the effort.

Children were crying. Women were screaming.

And above it all, Flynn was still yelling. 'No. No.' Raw fury. Unbearable pain.

The priest was on his knees, bending over Flynn's da who was groaning on the floor, his eyes wide with shock.

It felt like I stood there a lifetime, though it could only have been a few seconds. Nothing changed.

And then I knew what I had to do.

I walked closer to Flynn. His yells vibrated right through me. His face was purple, spit flying out of his mouth.

'No,' he yelled, still struggling against the men who held him.

Their shouts whirled around me. I focused on Flynn. He was completely out of control – his eyes wild and staring, looking through me. Not seeing me. My heart thumped frantically.

'No,' he roared.

I took a step closer, my whole body shaking.

Then I reached out, my arms outstretched, and took his face in my hands.

'No.' He tried to shake me off, still bellowing like an animal. But I kept my hands against his cheeks.

'Look at me,' I said.

He didn't hear me. Didn't even see me.

I walked closer, right up to him. I was completely certain that if the men holding him had let go, he would have punched me away from him, not even realising who I was.

I stood so close our noses were almost touching. I could feel the heat and the rage bouncing off him in terrible, terrifying waves.

'Look at me,' I repeated. I wasn't shouting, but I was so close to him now that he had to hear.

His eyes were pale gold. Wild with rage.

'Look at me,' I said.

At last he focused on me. The yell died on his lips. I saw him register who I was. I stared steadily at him.

'Come back,' I whispered.

13

Flynn stopped struggling. For a long moment he stared at me. Then he closed his eyes and sagged forwards, resting his face against the side of my head.

The men around us stopped yelling. Siobhan stopped screaming. I put my arms round Flynn's spent body. The church was still full of shouting and crying, but Flynn was silent. The men let go of him. He wrapped his arms around me, his head now heavy on my shoulder.

We stood there. Then I felt a hand on my back.

'Let's get him out of here.' It was Gary. I let him guide me towards the door, as I half steered, half supported Flynn.

The sunlight hit me as we walked outside. I looked sideways up at Gary.

'Wait here a minute.' Gary disappeared back inside.

Flynn straightened up. He looked away, but I

caught the sunlight glistening on his face, wet with tears. His whole body was shaking.

'River?' he choked. 'Please. I don't . . . I can't . . .'

I knew what he wanted. Without saying anything, I gripped his hand and ran, pulling him along the pavement. After a couple of steps Flynn broke into a run. Immediately he was faster than me, dragging me behind him.

We ran hard down the street, took a left, then a couple of rights.

At last we turned onto a small patch of grass: a sort of mini-park with a few trees. It was deserted. Flynn slowed to a walk and led me over to one of the trees. He slumped down, still holding my hand, pulling me down beside him.

He hung his head, his shaking hand holding mine tightly in my lap. I knew he was crying and not wanting me to see his face. I knelt up, let go of his hand and took him in my arms.

He curled over, his head against me, sobbing.

I held him until he stopped. Then I took his face in my hands and lifted it.

'Oh,' I gasped. Before, in the church, I'd only focused on his eyes. But now I saw that his lip was split and that a dark red bruise bloomed on his chin. 'You're hurt.' I looked down. Flynn's shirt was torn and smeared with blood.

He turned his head away and wiped his eyes. I waited, my heart in my mouth, not knowing what to say.

At last Flynn cleared his throat. 'I wanted to kill him,' he said, dully. 'If I'd had a knife . . .' He gulped.

A chill ran down my spine. His raging, terrifying face flashed in front of my eyes. 'But you didn't,' I said quickly. 'Your dad was okay. I saw his face, his eyes were open, he was moving.'

Flynn stared at me, then sat back, against the tree. 'I don't know . . .' He stopped.

I waited. 'Don't know what?' I said.

He looked at me, his expressive face so torn with misery that I could hardly breathe.

'I don't know anything,' he whispered. 'I don't know who I am. I don't know anything. Just . . .' He took my hand. '. . . just that you're the only thing that makes sense.'

I looked down at his hand. The knuckles were ripped raw, bleeding.

'We should go to a hospital,' I said. 'Make sure you're okay.'

Flynn shook his head. 'No.' He leaned his forehead down on mine. 'Please don't leave,' he whispered. 'Please don't go away.'

I kissed his bruised mouth gently. My heart was so full it felt like it was bursting.

'I'm not going away,' I whispered. 'Not ever.'

He put his arms round me and we sat back against the tree. We sat there for a long time, just holding each other.

The sun went behind a cloud. Flynn shivered. I drew away from him. 'Please let's go down to the hospital,' I said. 'Your hand looks awful and you've got all those cuts on your face.'

Flynn shook his head again. 'Maybe Goldbar's,' he said. 'There's an old guy there who's a physio.'

I reluctantly agreed.

It took about twenty minutes to get to Goldbar's. We walked in silence most of the way. Now the initial shock of what had happened was over, my mind was racing. It was like the whole world had shifted. All the other things that had happened to me and Flynn were nothing compared to what I'd seen today, to how out of control he'd been. I didn't know somebody could be like that. I didn't know someone could have so much hate inside them.

It changed everything. It didn't matter how often I told myself that his da *hadn't* been killed. Or that he deserved all that anger. The truth was that if those guys hadn't pulled him away, Flynn could have – probably would have – killed his own father. Not because he'd really hurt me or Caitlin. And not in self-defence. But because years of hurt and rage and guilt had built up inside him, waiting to explode.

We got to Goldbar's just before three. Flynn walked straight past the guy reading his paper, not even bothering to speak to him. He dragged me down the concrete corridor and into the room with the boxing rings.

I steeled myself for looks and comments. But the room was practically empty. Just a couple of young guys punching at one of the bags. An older man I recognised from before was squatting near the door, checking something in a cupboard. He looked up and did a double take as he took in Flynn's face and bloodstained shirt. He strode over.

'Flynn?' he said. 'What happened to you, lad?'

Flynn held up his hand.

'Crikey.' The old guy glanced at me.

'This is River,' Flynn said. 'River, this is John.'

John nodded at me, then led Flynn over to the corner of the room. 'Come on then, son. Let me have a look.'

John took a first aid box out of the cupboard. He pressed his palm down on Flynn's shoulder, pushing him into a chair. I stood beside them as John examined Flynn's hand and checked out the cuts and bruises on his face.

'I thought you took the day off to go to church?' John said with a grin.

'That's where we were,' I said.

John glanced at me with raised eyebrows. Then he looked back at Flynn and picked a bandage out of the box.

'So what does the other geezer look like?'

Flynn looked up. 'Mashed.' He grinned.

What? How had he gone from all that earlier fear and pain to this . . . this macho rubbish?

'Flynn.' I almost stamped my foot. 'It's not a joke.'

John shook his head at me. He started winding the bandage round Flynn's hand.

'Who was it?'

'His dad,' I said quickly.

'Your old man?' John threw Flynn a knowing look. 'Well, I guess he had that coming.'

I blinked.

'You're fine. Nothing broken.' John looked over at a stream of men pouring into the room. 'Training session's about to start.' He fished a T-shirt and a pair of old sweatpants out of the box at his side. 'You want to join in?'

'Yes,' Flynn said.

'No,' I snapped at the same time.

Flynn took the sweats and moved towards the

other men. I put out my hand to stop him. John caught my arm. He winked at me.

Flynn walked off.

'What are—?'

'Listen, sweetheart,' John grunted. 'It's what he needs.'

I frowned. 'What are you *talking* about? He's just been in a fight. He's hurt . . .'

'I know.' John smiled at me. 'That's why he needs this. It's order. It's discipline. It's something to get his head round. Why d'you think he came here?'

I stared at him.

'Flynn's a good kid. I've known him for years. Knew his old man too. Used to come round here a lot. He brought Flynn his first few times. Back when he was ten or eleven.' He sighed. 'You could always see Patrick Hayes was a loser.'

'How does that make it right for Flynn to be doing a training session right now?' I felt bewildered. In my world Flynn needed to be held, comforted.

Someone on the other side of the room was calling everyone together.

The old guy sighed. 'Flynn's a determined kid.' He glanced at me. 'He's trying to turn out okay. Against all the odds.'

I frowned.

The man across the room was barking out orders now. 'Run. Jump. Thirty jacks. Thirty press-ups.'

I watched Flynn doing press-ups. His face was impassive, though surely his bandaged hand *had* to be hurting him. At least no one seemed to have noticed me, shrunk away in the corner. I tugged my jacket round me and sank into a chair.

I didn't get it. I didn't get it at all.

14

The man, whose name was Andy, kept the whole group on their toes. He told them to divide into pairs, then yelled, 'Jab. Jab. Hook. Uppercut. Jab. Cross.'

As the men started swinging at each other, Andy wandered around the room, barking out orders.

'Keep your guard up. Retract that punch. Thirty press-ups. Come *on*, ladies.'

I watched, appalled, as the men in the room sweated and fought their way through half an hour of boxing exercises. They were supposed to block each other's punches – but some got through. A couple of times I saw guys flying to the floor. Apart from the press-ups, the only respite from the fighting was when Andy told them to run the length of the room. The discipline was ferocious. Anyone who didn't do exactly as directed was singled out for ridicule and punishment. I noticed that this was never Flynn and marvelled. The boy who would be rude to his teachers and my mum and all our friends if they so much as looked weirdly at him, meekly doing what he was told. For thirty minutes straight.

I got a few comments and sniggers, but nothing compared to the other day. At the end Flynn panted over to me. His face was covered in sweat but his eyes were shining. I shook my head. John had been right. Flynn looked way better than he had done before the training session.

'Everything make sense again?' I asked drily.

It didn't make sense to me. Flynn was incredibly bright. He was a super-subtle actor and unbelievably sensitive in so many ways. And yet he was into all this too – this structured violence that I couldn't see the point of.

He grinned down at me. 'I told you,' he said. '*You're* the only thing that makes sense.' The smile on his face faded. He looked anxious. 'Will you come with me to James's? I know you like it there. I don't want to go home yet. I just want to be with you.'

A warm glow spread through me. I might not understand Flynn as well as I'd like but the way we felt about each other was what really counted. It put everything else in the shadows.

Flynn changed out of the sweats and back into his shirt and trousers. We walked out together and got a bus to James's house. James opened the door, staring at the sight of Flynn's cut face and bloodstained shirt.

'What happened?'

'Fight at Goldbar's,' Flynn mumbled.

A sceptical look flickered across James's face.

Flynn looked him in the eye. 'Okay, there wasn't,' he said. 'But we need somewhere to hide out for the night anyway.'

James hesitated for a second. He glanced at me, then back at Flynn. 'Right,' he nodded. 'Come on.'

He checked his parents wouldn't be home for another couple of hours, then took us up to the little spare room. He brought Flynn a fresh T-shirt then left us, saying he had to go and have his dinner.

Flynn went into the little room next door to have a shower. I'd switched off my phone as soon as Flynn and I had run away from the church. I turned it on again. Ignoring the missed calls and messages, I texted Mum and told her I wasn't coming home that night. I knew she'd be mad. I didn't care. All I cared about was Flynn.

I lay down on the bed. The silky blue bedspread and matching curtains were somehow comforting.

I closed my eyes, willing myself to relax, but I couldn't slow my mind down. Flynn's raging face forced its way into my head again. I shivered, trying to push the image away. I didn't want to face up to what his anger meant. To how afraid I'd been of him.

After a few minutes Flynn emerged from the bathroom, damp-haired, a towel around his middle. He sat down next to me on the bed. The bruises on his face were darkening and his lip was swollen. I reached over and held his bandaged fist in my hand.

'Thank you,' Flynn said.

I looked up. 'What for?'

'For staying,' he said softly. He leaned down and kissed me, very gently, on the cheek.

We lay next to each other in silence. After a few minutes, Flynn rolled onto his side and looked at me.

'I know you're worried about how angry I got . . . get . . .' he said.

I stared at him. 'You have to do something about it.'

'I know.' Flynn cleared his throat. 'I will.' He paused. His eyes – intense and gold in the lamplight – glistened. 'I've never cried like that in front of anyone before.'

I stroked his face, my finger tracing the outline of his cut lip.

'I don't want to go back out there,' he said quietly. 'I just want this. To be here with you.'

I rested my finger on his mouth. 'This can't last,' I said. 'Your mum will be worried. You'll have to face school. I'll have to face my parents.'

Flynn looked at me, his eyes all soft. 'That stuff with my da,' he said. 'That's got nothing to do with how I feel about you.'

'I know,' I said steadily. 'But it still . . . it . . . it still has an impact. Look at earlier today, when you got angry with me for not telling you about Siobhan's boyfriend.'

'I know.' Flynn's face fell. 'I dunno why I got so mad. It's just the idea of someone else hurting Siobhan . . . I know I wasn't being fair, I'm sorry.'

I nodded, feeling nervous about what I was going to say . . . of how he would react. 'Sometimes I wonder if you get so angry because . . . because you're scared.'

I braced myself, waiting for the familiar look of fury to blaze out of Flynn's eyes. But to my surprise he just held my gaze, his face inexpressibly sad.

'I wonder that too,' he said very quietly. 'It's like . . . I'm scared I won't be able to protect you. I couldn't take it . . . you being hurt. You, Siobhan, Mum, Caitlin . . .'

'Or yourself,' I whispered. *'You're* scared of being hurt too, so you push people away before it can happen.'

'Oh, Riv.' Flynn stroked his hand through my hair. Deep creases lined his forehead. 'Sometimes it feels like it's you and me against the world.'

'Sssh.' We lay on the bed for a long time, just gazing into each other's eyes. Eventually, it grew dusky outside. I closed my eyes, feeling exhausted. I turned around, nestling into Flynn. I pulled his arm over me, letting myself sink back into him, letting myself fall. I couldn't think anymore. All I wanted to do was sleep.

When I woke, it was dark. I sat up, taking a moment to adjust to the gloom. Flynn was lying on his side facing away from me, his hair flopping over his face. I was still dressed, but he had pulled the covers over me. I wriggled closer and he turned into me, still asleep, his arm reaching out, pulling me closer. I snuggled up next to him, vaguely wondering what James had said to his parents and how my mum had felt about my text saying I wasn't coming home that night. Then Flynn snuffled into my hair. And I fell asleep again.

It was light when I woke next. Flynn's arm was

still over me. I could tell it was early, but I felt wide awake. I lifted his arm, got out of bed and wandered over to the window. The sun was already high in the sky. I checked the time. Almost eight-thirty a.m. on Monday morning. A school day. School felt like a million miles from what Flynn and I had lived through this weekend.

'River?'

I turned round. Flynn was staring blearily up at me.

'We should leave before James's parents see us,' I said. 'It's going to be so embarrassing when—'

'Relax.' Flynn smiled sleepily. 'James came up after you'd gone to sleep. His folks have no idea we're here. They've gone to work now. James has left too. I heard them. James said your mum called last night, asking if we were here, but James told her no.' He took a deep breath. 'I explained about my da – he'd more or less guessed anyway. Let's stay here for a bit longer, Riv, yeah?'

'What about school?' I wandered over and stood beside the bed.

He raised his eyebrows. 'What about it?'

My eyes widened. 'You're considering *not going*? What about your A levels? What about Mr *I'm working hard to become a lawyer and stomp on the poor people*?'

'What about giving the other kids a chance to catch up?' he said with a grin. Then his face fell. 'Seriously, I don't want to have to deal with school today.'

'You think they'll know about . . . what happened at the church?'

'For sure.'

I stared at the dark bruises around his mouth. 'We have to face everyone at some point.'

'Okay, but not now.'

I looked at the fierce heat in his eyes. At his bruised face. At the knots of muscle along his arms. What was Mum going to say when she knew that Flynn had beaten up his da? What would Flynn's da do? And what about Flynn's school?

'I don't want to face it all either,' I whispered. We spent the next few hours making out. It was strange but, despite my not really understanding how Flynn could be so full of hate towards his dad, I felt closer to him than ever. We even talked, again, about taking things further between us. I told Flynn how I felt – that I was sure I would be ready soon, that I just needed a little more time.

In the end, hunger drove us out of the room. James had brought up some bread the night before, but Flynn had eaten most of that before he'd gone to sleep and I was starving. We tidied the little bedroom then crept downstairs for juice and cereal.

'James has been brilliant, hasn't he?' I said as we sat in the kitchen. 'He's a really good friend.'

Flynn looked up. 'Don't start fancying him, will you?' He smiled.

I rolled my eyes. 'I'm just saying . . .' I paused. 'I wish you liked Grace more,' I said tentatively.

Flynn frowned. He rolled his glass against his swollen lip. 'I do like Grace,' he said. 'She's nice . . . kind. And James loves her. He told me.'

I grinned, thinking how pleased Grace would be to hear that. 'He said that?'

'Course. Last year, he went on and on about her for weeks. In the end I practically had to force him to promise me he'd talk to her at that party where you puked up.'

'It's funny but I thought back then he fancied Emmi,' I said, remembering the early *Romeo and Juliet* rehearsals.

'He did,' Flynn said, spooning up some cereal.

I shook my head. 'But how . . . ?'

'Come on, Riv. It's possible to fancy more than one person at once, you know.'

I looked at him. 'Not for me,' I said.

We finished our cereal, lost in our own thoughts. Flynn washed up the bowls while I put the juice and milk back in the fridge. The doorbell rang. A single, persistent chime. We looked at each other. I rushed to the kitchen window.

A police car was parked outside. My stomach turned over.

'Feds?' Flynn said in a flat voice.

I gulped. 'Yes.'

The doorbell rang on. 'What do we do?' I said.

I don't know what I expected Flynn to say – maybe that he was going to make a run for it out the back. But to my surprise he just stood up, calm as anything. 'I'll let them in,' he said. 'I'll make it clear you don't know anything . . . that there's no point them speaking to you.'

The doorbell was still ringing, its sound piercing through my skull.

'You knew they would come,' I said, realising how naïve I'd been not thinking this would happen. Someone in the church was bound to have called the police when the fight started. There were only a few places Flynn would hide out after all. It wouldn't take that long for the police to check all of them.

Flynn walked out into the hall. I followed him, my legs trembling.

Flynn opened the front door. I just caught a flash of blue uniforms before Flynn stepped outside, pulling the door shut behind him.

I raced over and opened it. Two young, male police officers glanced at me, then back at Flynn.

'We're looking for a Patrick Flynn?' one of them said. He looked at the picture in his hand, then up at Flynn again. 'That you?'

'Yes, sir,' Flynn said in a meek voice.

And then the police officer arrested him.

15

I got home just before midday. After the police had seen me at James's house, they'd taken my name and phone number and warned me that I'd be needed later to make a statement. Then they'd marched Flynn off to the police station. They were very polite but they were still acting like he was a criminal.

My head spun with the implications of this.

All I wanted to do was get up to my bedroom and lie on my bed for a bit. With any luck my younger brother Stone wouldn't be home for hours. And Mum shouldn't be back from work until at least six. It was too much to hope that she wouldn't give me a grilling over where I'd been last night and today, but at least I'd have a few hours to try and wind down.

No such luck. As I crept in through the front door, Mum, Dad and Dad's girlfriend Gemma all emerged from the kitchen. They stared at me in silence. Mum cleared her throat. I braced myself, waiting for her to explode, but she didn't say anything, just looked at me, her expression a weird mix of relief, frustration and misery. With a twinge of guilt I realised there were dark shadows under her eyes and her face looked unnaturally pale.

Dad strode across the hall and pulled me into an enormous hug. 'Oh, River,' he said. 'Thank goodness you're safe.'

'Of course I'm safe.' I hugged him back, breathing in his smell of incense and musty clothes. 'I texted Mum last night. What are you doing here?'

Dad drew back. Above his beard his skin looked even more weatherbeaten than usual. His expression was as miserable as Mum's. Gemma appeared at his shoulder. Her long black hair was tied back in a ponytail and she was wearing a blue top that brought out the colour of her eyes. She smiled at me then touched Dad lightly on the arm. 'I'll wait in the living room.'

She disappeared through the door, shutting it behind her.

Dad led me into the kitchen. Mum followed. She still hadn't said anything.

'Sit down, River,' Dad said.

I sat opposite him and Mum at the table. 'What's going on?' I asked.

'What's going on?' Mum hissed, breaking her silence at last. 'You run away with your criminally violent boyfriend, stay out all night and don't bother to show up at school, and you're asking what's going on?'

'We were worried,' Dad said. '*Really* worried. The police came round earlier looking for Flynn. They thought he might be with you. Can you imagine how terrified we felt not knowing where you were?'

My mouth fell open. In as far as I'd thought about it at all, I hadn't imagined for a moment that my parents would get this anxious about me.

'But I sent a text, Mum,' I said. 'I'm really sorry I didn't go to school today. I won't do it ever again. It was just all a bit heavy for Flynn yesterday and—'

'Heavy for *Flynn*?' Mum jumped up from the table. She turned to Dad, gesticulating wildly. 'D'you see what I mean? He's totally brainwashed her.' She turned back to me. 'Your precious Flynn nearly killed his own father yesterday, River. He beat his face to a pulp. He broke his nose.'

I stared at her. Flynn's da's face covered in blood flashed back into my mind. I felt sick.

'You don't know what Flynn's dad did to him.' I gripped the table between us. 'What he did to their whole family.'

Dad put his hand on mine. 'We do know, River.

We spoke to Flynn's mum yesterday. She told us something of what happened in the past . . .'

'If I'd known, I would *never* have let you get mixed up with him . . .' Mum shouted.

Dad held up his hand to stop her. 'The point is that even his own mother admits he's out of control,' he said. 'That there was no—'

'His dad was frightening Caitlin,' I said, my heart in my throat. I couldn't believe Dad was backing Mum against me.

'For God's sake, River!' Mum yelled, red-faced.

'Listen.' Dad's voice was low and serious. 'The police have a church full of witnesses who all say that what Flynn did was unprovoked. That *he* was the aggressive one.'

My hands shook as I thought about the serious-faced young officer who'd arrested Flynn earlier.

'As far as we could work out from what the police said, there are no plans to charge him yet and the lawyer at Gemma's therapy centre thinks there's a good chance that won't happen, but it's still very serious.'

'You mean prison?' I gasped.

'No, that's not what I'm saying. The background with his dad, the grades he's getting at school and his potential are all in his favour. But the police will want to make him realise there are consequences.'

131

'He *should* be sent to prison,' Mum snapped. 'He's totally out of control.'

'But—'

'No, River.' Mum folded her arms. 'This is the last straw. Since you met him everything's gone wrong. You're not working properly at school. Bunking off today proves it.'

'But I *am* working,' I protested. 'Today was . . . different.'

'It's not just that,' Mum went on. 'You hardly spend any time with your other friends. You've lied to me. Stayed out all night. More than once. It has to stop.'

I stared at Dad. 'You can't . . .'

A pained expression came into Dad's eyes. 'The last thing I want to do is forbid you to do something. I feel guilty that I haven't been more involved up till now. That things have got this far.'

Mum snorted.

'But Flynn's good for me,' I protested. 'Okay so he's got a temper, but he's sweet and kind when he's on his own and—'

'You can't be sure he won't hurt you,' Dad said.

'He'd *never* hurt me.' Tears welled up in my eyes. 'He hasn't hurt anyone else. Don't you understand? Flynn hates what his dad did. He only ever gets angry with *him*. About *him*.'

132

'What about the fights he's been getting into at school?' Dad said gently. 'His mum admitted he's always being disciplined for rudeness. Always pushing things. I mean, he was even suspended from school the other day.'

'I know, and he knows that he overreacts to things . . .'

'He needs therapy,' Dad said. 'A proper, intensive course of anger management. The kind of thing they do at Gemma's centre. There are places all over London, some of them actually specialise in adolescent aggression.'

'But Flynn's not really aggressive,' I insisted. 'Not deep down. He's just scared of being hurt. Of people he loves being hurt. That's why he loses his temper sometimes but he can stop himself, at—'

Dad took my hand across the table. 'You're not listening, River. You *know*. In your heart you *know* I'm right. Whatever Flynn says, it's not that easy to just "stop". And violence is *never* the answer to an argument. Maybe sometimes in self-defence you have to take a stand, but Flynn goes way too far, way too often.'

I pulled my hand away from his and stood up. The tiny silver heart on my bracelet dangled against my wrist, a reminder of Flynn and what we shared together. My parents just didn't understand.

'You were happy enough that he hit those guys who were all over me and Emmi last term,' I said, remembering how Flynn had fended off two guys hassling us last December.

'I wonder if we got the full story about that,' Mum said drily.

'So now I'm a liar?'

'No, River,' Dad said. 'That's not what we're saying.'

Mum crossed her arms. 'It's not just the violence. Flynn's been accused of stealing things. Emmi's mother told us all about Alex's iPad going missing at school. It sounds like all the evidence points to Flynn and—'

'He didn't do anything. They're just blaming him because they don't like him.' Tears leaked out of my eyes. I didn't even bother to brush them away. Mum *and* Dad were both against me. Against Flynn. 'You can't stop me seeing him,' I sobbed.

'Then you have to move out,' Mum said, simply. 'Because I can't live like this anymore.'

'Move out?' I whispered. It felt like the floor was falling away from underneath me.

Dad took my hand. 'You can come and live with me and Gemma on the commune.'

'But . . . but . . . ?' My mind whirled with the ramifications of this. Dad's commune was a ninety-minute drive from here – way more in rush hour. 'What about school? What about my GSCEs?'

Dad swallowed. 'I realise it's not an ideal time for you to move schools with your exams coming up but there are other schools near the commune where—'

'What about my friends?' I stared at both of them. I couldn't believe they were seriously suggesting I should leave my whole life behind, just to get me away from Flynn.

'Oh,' Mum said sarcastically. 'So *now* you care about your friends?'

'Look, River,' Dad said. 'We both know you coming to live with me at this point isn't the best thing for you. We're only suggesting it if you refuse to stop seeing Flynn of your own accord. Neither of us can be here twenty-four hours a day to watch over you so we need you to promise you'll end things with him.'

'No.' The word blurted out of me. Not seeing Flynn was unthinkable. Impossible.

'Then you have to go where you *can't* see him,' Mum said.

'It's your choice, River,' Dad said. 'But you do have to choose. We both care too much about you to let things carry on as they are.'

'You're grounded for a fortnight either way,' Mum added.

I looked at them, feeling desperate. 'What if Flynn apologises? What if we just see each other a couple of times a week? No staying over and—'

'He's not good for you,' Mum said sternly. 'Look at yesterday. He didn't even stop to see if his father was all right. He just ran off, dragging you with him.'

I opened my mouth to explain that wasn't how it happened. Then I shut it again. I could see on both their faces that I wasn't going to change their minds. They were as prejudiced against Flynn as everyone else.

They were going to force me to choose – to stay here without Flynn, or live on the commune with Dad, also without Flynn.

'You can have tonight to think about it,' Dad said. 'Gemma and I are staying with friends nearby. We'll come back in the morning and you can tell us what you've decided.'

I turned and ran up to my room.

It was no choice. No life.

No life without Flynn.

16

I tried to speak to Flynn that evening but his phone was switched off, so I called Emmi. She and Grace had both been trying to get hold of me all day. Before I could even explain the terrible situation my parents had put me in, Emmi jumped in with her own news. She'd heard about Flynn's arrest through Alex. Apparently the news had already spread right through the boys' school.

'But that's not all,' she said. I could hear the horrified excitement in her voice and realised, with a miserable twist in my gut, that she was enjoying the drama.

'What's not all?' I said.

'One of the guys in their year *saw* Flynn with Alex's iPad. He posted on Facebook saying so.'

'Then he's lying,' I said. But inside I wasn't entirely sure. Maybe Flynn *had* taken the iPad. Everyone knew he hated Alex, plus there was that silver

137

bracelet. Anyway, how could I know what he was capable of? Until yesterday I wouldn't have thought he could attack his dad like he had.

'Wake up, River,' Emmi said. 'I know how you feel about him. I'm only saying it because I care about you but . . .' she paused.

'*But?*' I said angrily.

'But Flynn's totally out of control,' she went on. 'Alex reckons they'll exclude him for good for what happened at the church.'

'No,' I gasped. 'They couldn't. What about his A levels?'

Emmi sucked in her breath. 'Guess he should have thought of that before getting into endless fights.'

I sighed. She was never going to understand how complicated Flynn was . . . how difficult his life had been . . . I decided to change the subject. 'Hey, Em, you're not going to believe what my mum and dad want me to do.'

Emmi squealed with horror as I told her they were on the verge of sending me to live on Dad's commune. 'I have to say I'll stop seeing Flynn or Mum will chuck me out.'

'Then there's no contest.' For Emmi, the decision was obvious. 'You have to stay here. I mean there's no Flynn, either way. And at least if you stay you can keep coming to our school where all your friends are.'

'I guess,' I said.

'And if you stay here, maybe you can still see Flynn sometimes. You know, when your Mum's out and stuff.'

Was Emmi encouraging me to keep the relationship going? 'I thought you'd think it was a good thing if we split up,' I said, feeling confused.

There was a short silence on the other end of the phone.

'Yeah, well, maybe it would be,' Emmi said. 'But I know how you feel about each other.'

'Really?'

Emmi sighed. 'River, anyone with half a brain cell can see it. What you two have, it's rare. Like that time last December, just before those two guys attacked us. I remember looking at you, the way he pulled you closer and you shivered, you looked . . . I dunno . . . ecstatic. And he was running his hand down your face and looking at you like you were his whole life. Not even aware of anyone else in the room.'

I remembered that specific moment only vaguely, but I knew what Emmi was describing – those moments where everything else in the world faded away and it was just me and Flynn.

'So yes, rationally, I think you'd be better off without him,' Emmi went on, 'but for all his arrogance and his moods, he adores you and you adore him and right now I can't see either of you surviving being apart.'

I couldn't get hold of Flynn that night. But in the end it didn't matter. I made the only decision I could. I told Mum I would stay with her, and keep going to school, and that I wouldn't see Flynn. I told her I was truly sorry for all the pain I'd caused her. That I accepted I was grounded for two weeks. And that I would work really hard for my GCSEs over the next few months.

I meant it – every bit of it. Except the part about not seeing Flynn. I knew I would have to be careful, but somehow I was going to see him again.

I had to. Like Emmi said, I would die if I didn't.

The next day – Tuesday – Mum packed me off to school explaining she expected me home straight afterwards. She also announced she wanted to see the call log on my phone every day so she could check I wasn't speaking with Flynn. She had already made me delete my Facebook account.

But it's basically impossible to stop two people talking if that's what they want to do. I spent a long, humiliating ten minutes being lectured by the head for missing school the day before, but at last I was free. I borrowed Grace's mobile and called Flynn at school. To my intense relief he answered straight away. Not that he told me much about what had happened to him when he got back from the police station on Sunday. Just that – as Dad predicted – he wasn't being charged.

'And my dad's fine – apart from his nose it's just a few bruises.'

I explained what Mum and Dad had said to me. There was a long silence on the other end of the phone.

'That sucks, Riv,' he said at last.

I'd expected him to insist that I had to lie to my parents and do anything I could to keep seeing him, but he was strangely silent.

'What do you think I should do?' I asked in the end.

'Let me think about it, yeah?'

What? In all the time I'd known him, I'd never heard Flynn hesitate for more than a few seconds before announcing his views. He always knew his own mind.

'Okay,' I said, thrown. I raised the outstanding question that was still in my head. 'Emmi told me there was someone at your school who claims he saw you with Alex's iPad. Did the police ask about that?'

Flynn gave a derisive growl. 'Yeah, they asked. But that guy doesn't know what he saw. Anyway, even if he saw me holding an iPad – which he didn't because I wasn't – there's no proof it was Alex's. The whole thing is just his word against mine.' He paused. 'You do believe me about that, don't you, Riv?'

'Course,' I said. But, once again, a shard of doubt lodged itself in my mind. 'So, you're not being chucked out of school . . . or sent to prison?' I said, trying to cover my confusion.

'No, but . . .' Flynn hesitated. In the distance I could hear the bell ringing at his school, signalling the end of break. 'There's something I need to talk to you about. Can I meet you after school? I'll be careful no one sees me.'

'Okay,' I said, my heart beating faster. What on earth did Flynn want to talk about that he couldn't say over the phone?

I was in a state, waiting to see him, all day. I couldn't concentrate on any of my lessons. Flynn clearly had something important to tell me and I was terrified of what it might be. He hadn't been charged by the police and his school had obviously decided to give

142

him another chance. Apart from my parents' ulti-matum, nothing between us was really that different from how it had been last week. Was it?

I raced out of school as soon as the bell rang. Flynn was already there, leaning against the end of the metal-barred gate. Everything about him was so perfect. The way he stood, the way his whole body fitted together. I moved closer. The bruises on his face had come out properly now – dark purple and grey. I stared, soaking him up. A moment later he turned, saw me looking, and smiled.

'You look a mess,' I said, walking over.

'I know.' He put his arms around me and held me. Girls were starting to trickle out of the gate now. A couple passed us, giggling. 'Come on, let's get out of here before anyone sees us and reports back to your mum.' Flynn took my hand and we strolled along the road. I leaned against him and he slid his arm around my shoulders. Again, I had that sense of us fitting together like we'd been made for each other. Being with Flynn was the best thing in my life. How could I possibly stop seeing him?

'So, what did you want to talk to me about?' I said.

Flynn looked across the road, away from me. My chest tightened.

'You're breaking your promise to your mum and

dad by being with me, aren't you?' he said, his voice flat and dull.

'That doesn't matter,' I said.

'Yes, it does.' Flynn paused, still staring into the distance. 'And, unless you agree to stop seeing me, you're going to be exiled to your dad's drop-out centre – which will take you away from your school and your friends too.'

'It's a commune, not a drop-out centre,' I said. 'But no way am I going there. And they can't stop me seeing you. Not if it's what we both want. Nobody else understands us – like *no one*. So they don't understand that we're going to find a way to be together. We *have* to . . .' I stopped.

Flynn turned back to look at me. His whole face was etched with misery.

'What is it?' Fear twisted inside me.

We turned the corner onto a quieter, smaller road. We were just three streets from my house. Flynn stopped walking. He rested his hands on my waist and dipped his head down to touch mine.

'I've screwed up, River,' he whispered. 'I don't mean just Sunday. I mean . . . I mean everything.'

I stared up at him, a hard lump in my throat. Flynn closed his eyes and rolled his forehead across mine. For a second I wondered if he was going to admit to stealing Alex's iPad, but then he said,

'When I got home from the police station it was awful. You should have seen the state Mum was in. I've never seen her like that. Siobhan said she'd been hysterical since . . . what happened in the church. I couldn't bear it . . . Mum's always so together and here she was, all upset, and it was my fault. And then Siobhan was angry with me for what I did and for running off afterwards.' He stopped and his voice dropped to almost a whisper. 'But the worst thing was Caitlin. She . . . oh, River . . . she was frightened of me. When I went near her she shrank away, like I might hit her or something. Just like she did when Da tried to touch her, remember?'

I nodded, stroking his bruised face. He opened his eyes. They were bright green, full of remorse. 'Mum wanted me to go to see a doctor cos of my face and I said there was no need. And then she started shouting at me. And I ended up shouting back which I didn't mean to . . . Anyway, she kept going on about the police, how they might charge me after all, how the school might exclude me . . . how I was throwing away all the chances I'd worked so hard for . . . Like I didn't know.' He paused.

'What happened next?' I said.

'I lost my temper with her and shouted that it wasn't fair to blame me, that it was Da's fault. And I

145

could see Siobhan in the corner of the room with her arms round Caitlin and they were both crying.' He screwed up his face. 'All three of them were crying. And it suddenly hit me, I'd turned into my da – like you told me once, remember? When we were doing the play?'

I nodded, my heart in my mouth.

'Well, suddenly I saw it too,' he said, his voice so low I could barely hear him. 'I saw myself – yelling and lashing out and scaring people. And I just stopped. I was so shocked that I just stopped. I don't even know what I was saying – I didn't say anything else. I just said sorry to Mum – for everything. And she hugged me and I let her but all I could think was that I was such a loser. And I *knew* how your folks would react. And if you were my daughter I'd feel the same way. So . . . so all I could think was . . . I've ruined everything. *Everything.*'

'No you haven't.' I pressed my hands gently against his face. 'I'm still here,' I said. 'I love you.'

'But just seeing me means you're breaking your word to your mum and dad.' Flynn drew back. 'I shouldn't be putting you in a position where—'

'Flynn, stop it,' I said. 'Stop worrying about everyone else. I'm choosing this. I'm choosing to see you because I know that Mum and Dad have got you wrong. Okay, so you've got a temper . . .'

'Riv, I could have killed him.' Flynn's eyes were darker, more urgent. 'You know that. The police kept saying it too. But what I realised . . . what really got to me when I saw Mum and the police and everyone . . . was that I don't honestly think I'd care if I had.' The words tumbled out of him, jerky and harsh. 'I can't help it, Riv. They're all going on about me doing therapy. Taking stupid anger management classes. And I'm, like, *yeah, yeah, you're right*. But the truth is that I've only been pretending to everyone that I'm sorry I hurt him, because really I'm not sorry at all. And you're the only one I can tell.' His voice cracked. 'I know it's wrong but he's a bastard and I hate him and I've always hated him . . .' He closed his eyes again.

I pulled him towards me and we hugged in silence. My heart pounded as Flynn's angry, raging face flashed into my head again. I tried to make sense of what he was saying. He hated his father. He didn't care if he killed him. I couldn't get my head round feelings like those. I simply couldn't imagine hating anyone that much, especially my own dad, no matter what he'd done.

'Maybe therapy *would* help?' I suggested timidly.

'No.' Flynn shook his head emphatically. 'No way. It's only my da who makes me that angry and I can deal with him.' He smiled. 'Anyway, I've got you to talk to.'

I sighed. A moment or two passed. The sun went behind a cloud. I started to worry about getting home – about Mum checking the clock, maybe even getting in her car and driving about looking for me. But Flynn was still holding me tightly. I suddenly knew there was something he hadn't told me yet. I looked up. *Yes.* It was there in his eyes. 'What is it?' My heart raced.

Flynn's mouth trembled. 'Mum wants . . .' He paused, his voice hollow. 'She wants us – me and Siob and Caitlin and her – to move back to Ireland.'

17

'What?' I couldn't have heard him right. 'You mean move to the *country* Ireland?'

'Yes, back to where Mum comes from.' He sighed. 'She wants me away from here. Away from my da. She's scared there'll be another fight and this time the police won't let it go.'

'But . . . ?' My heart was cracking into pieces. Ireland was far away. Far too far away. It made Dad's commune look like a short stroll round the corner. 'You're serious?' I whispered.

Flynn nodded. His voice was flat and dull. 'Mum's been in touch with her sister and we're going to stay there while we find somewhere to live.'

I gulped. 'So . . . so it sounds like it's all sorted.'
Don't go. Don't leave me.

Flynn's forehead creased into a frown. 'I could refuse. I mean Mum will definitely go and Siobhan and Caitlin will go with her. But I'm seventeen. I could stay here. I could get a job. A *proper* job and—'

'But you'd have to leave school,' I said, thinking of all Flynn's ambitions and all his hard work for his A levels.

'I know,' he said miserably. 'Look, I have to choose, Riv. And I want to choose you. But I don't know if I should. I don't know what to do. Mum's terrified I'm going to get in real trouble if I stay. If I don't go with her she says she'll worry all the time.' He paused. 'And I'll worry about *her*, Riv.' He looked down at me, his eyes deeply troubled. 'I'll worry about all of them.'

I wrapped my arms round his neck and leaned against his chest. Then I reached up and kissed him. *I can't let you go.* I kissed him fiercely, with only one aim. To remind him how hot I was. To remind him how good we were together.

I felt his heart beat faster.

Yes. I had him. A sense of power surged through me.

'Maybe I could come with you?' I whispered, my lips brushing against his ear. I couldn't see that working at all, but I was playing for time, trying to decide whether to turn him on more, or whether to start crying. I know how awful – how ruthless – that sounds, but I felt like I was fighting for my life.

Lust or pity – which would keep him with me?

'River.' He pressed against me.

Well, the lust was working so far . . .

I kissed him again.

He groaned. 'Can you imagine what your folks will do if you run off to Ireland? They'll have Interpol after me.' He pulled me really tightly against him, running his hands down my back. 'I don't see how you can come too. But like I said, I could stay.'

I looked up at him. His eyes were bright green, just the faintest hint of gold, hungry for me.

'Yes,' I whispered. 'You could stay . . . you could . . .' I stopped, thinking through the reality of what it would mean for Flynn to remain in London: he wouldn't just have to leave school and get a job, he'd also have to find somewhere to live on his own.

Flynn bent his forehead down onto mine. 'I'll stay if you want me too. I'll go anywhere with you. I don't want to lose you.'

I hugged him hard, fighting with my conscience. I wanted to plead with him to stay, but the words died on my lips. I couldn't ask him to give up everything just for me. And that's what him staying in London – or us running away together – would mean.

We stood holding each other in silence for what

felt like ages. My phone vibrated in my bag – it was bound to be Mum, wondering why I hadn't come straight home.

There wasn't much time.

'River?' Flynn's voice shook. 'I don't know . . .'

I gazed up at his strong, sad, beautiful face and it was obvious what I had to do.

'Well *I* know,' I said. 'I know it would be *really* difficult getting by on your own. And I know you'd hate being without your family. So . . . you should go.'

Flynn said nothing.

'Ireland's not *that* far away,' I went on. 'I could get a job – maybe your job at Café Yazmina – and save up my money so I could visit you.'

Flynn squeezed me tighter. 'Sure, we could *both* save up. But it'd be ages before we could afford the ticket. And I can't imagine your mum and dad letting you come and visit me.'

'Well, maybe they'll calm down. Maybe in a few months.'

I couldn't believe what I was hearing myself say. I couldn't survive for more than a few days without Flynn. Forget lust and pity. Every cell in my body was telling me to throw myself at his feet. Beg him not to go. To tell him how lost I'd be, how pointless everything would be without him.

But I didn't do any of those things. Instead I took a good look at his face. There was something too old about his eyes. Like he'd been through more than he should have. A deep-down weariness from responsibilities that he'd carried too young, for too long.

As I stood there, I knew that I couldn't add to them.

I took a step away from him. Just a small step.

'What does Siobhan say?' I said evenly.

Flynn rolled his eyes. 'Actually, she's all excited about it. She's been talking to Gary.' He scowled. 'He says he wants to come with us. Use his dad's money to buy a salon that he and Siob can work in. I don't know. Mum's dead keen. Siob's dead keen. Caitlin's all up for it one minute, then all down about leaving her friends the next.'

He reached out and pulled me back towards him.

'I don't want to go back to St Cletus's now anyway,' he said. 'It was obvious today that everyone at school knows about my da being . . . what he is. And that stupid friend of Alex's posting that he'd seen me with the freakin' iPad means now *everyone* thinks I'm a thief as well as a thug. I mean *everyone*, not just Alex and his mates and the teachers.' He paused. 'They'll all be glad to see the back of me. Mum talked to the head this morning, told him her plan. Apparently he said that a fresh start would be the best thing for me. Course what he *really* meant was that he was glad he wouldn't have to deal with me anymore.'

'So when is your mum planning on leaving?' I asked.

Flynn shrugged. 'A week today,' he said.

'Next Tuesday?' I gasped. I couldn't help it. That was just seven days away. Too soon. I couldn't prepare myself that quickly.

'I know.' He groaned. 'I can't think about anything except being with you. Tell me what to do, Riv. I'll do whatever you say.'

I hesitated. This was agony. 'I told you, you should go,' I said, swallowing down the tears that threatened to rise inside me. 'I mean, if you stayed you'd be staying for me, but we'd have to sneak around behind my parents' backs so we wouldn't be able to see each other that much. And you'd have rent to pay which would be hard. Plus you'd worry about your mum and your sisters all the time, wouldn't you?'

He nodded.

'So, it's obvious,' I said. 'You have to go and I have to stay. And . . . and maybe in the future . . .' I stopped as tears clogged my throat.

Don't cry. Not in front of him.

'I ought to get home,' I said.

He shook his head.

'Yeah.' I swallowed hard, forcing down the tears. 'I'll call you. I'll get a new phone. One Mum doesn't know about.'

'I'll see you every day before I go, River.' He lifted my chin up and looked into my eyes. 'And then we can text each other. And speak and Skype whenever we can. And . . .'

I drew back, unable to breathe, unable to hold back my tears any longer.

'I have to go,' I said. I couldn't look at him again. I turned and fled down the street, my heart feeling like it was breaking into a million pieces.

18

Flynn met me from school and walked me home every day for the rest of the week except on Friday, when I went to Grace's house and met him there. I'd explained to Mum that Grace and I needed to spend a couple of hours on some drama GCSE coursework.

'All the relevant stuff is at hers,' I pleaded. 'Please let me go round. Grace's mum will be in. She can call you when I arrive.'

Mum reluctantly agreed and everything went according to plan. Grace's mum rung mine to confirm I was there, then Grace and I went upstairs to her room and called Flynn. He came over straight away. We let him in the back door and snuck him upstairs. Grace's mum had no idea.

Later, Grace went out to meet James and Flynn walked me home. We chatted away, hand in hand. Flynn was clearly relieved that the decision had been made. 'Mum's making all the arrangements,' he said. 'Her sister's sent the money and she's bought our tickets. We're flying to Dublin first thing Tuesday.'

'What about your job at the café?' I asked. 'Did you talk to Yazmina?'

'Yes, my job is yours if you want it,' Flynn said with a smile.

'Great.' I didn't feel much like smiling back right now, but this was good news. I liked the café and the Turkish lady who ran it very much.

'Yazmina says she'll talk to you about the job if you go round on Monday evening.'

'Will you be there too?' I asked.

'Try keeping me away.'

I talked to Mum about taking the Café Yazmina job that evening. I'd already promised her and Dad that my relationship with Flynn was over, of course, but she was still delighted to hear he was leaving the country. I said nothing in response, just pointed out that it meant Flynn's job at the café was available.

'It'll be good for me,' I said. 'And it's just a couple of evenings a week, Mum. It won't even get in the way of my schoolwork.'

Mum agreed to think about it. The next day was

Saturday. Dad arrived to pick up me and Stone mid-morning. We were spending the rest of the weekend at the commune. I didn't want to go. But what could I say? I only wanted to stay to see Flynn. And, right now, I was still grounded – not supposed to socialise with anyone, let alone him.

Once we arrived, I snuck down to the apple orchard to find a place with a signal – reception was rubbish at the commune – and called Flynn on a borrowed phone. We told each other what we'd been doing and how much we missed each other. But the conversation was all holes and spaces – it was what we weren't saying that was really important.

I can't bear that you're going away.

Stone and I got home late on Sunday night. My little brother had been surprisingly nice to me all weekend. I don't mean he asked how I was or anything, but he didn't tease me or call me any of his usual names.

Mum was as distant and subdued with me as normal. At least she said I could take the job at Café Yazmina, though she insisted that she'd have to pick me up from school the following afternoon and come with me to the café to meet Yazmina.

My heart sank. As Mum well knew, Monday was Flynn's last night in London. My final chance to say goodbye. I'd imagined our parting so many times, even wondering if this might be the moment when I chose to lose my virginity. After all, I wanted to make it special – and to ensure Flynn remembered how good we were together. But there'd be no way I'd be able to see him with Mum at my side from the school gates onwards. I could have skipped school entirely, but that would have definitely led to Mum banning me from taking the café job. And I was going to need that job to earn the money to visit Flynn in Ireland.

Monday evening arrived. I'd told Flynn earlier (using Grace's phone) that I didn't think I'd be able to see him. He hadn't said much – just promised that if I couldn't get away he would call the next day, as soon as they arrived in Dublin. It wasn't enough. I couldn't bear the idea of not being able to say goodbye – but what could I do? True to her word, Mum was waiting when I walked out of school and we spent the next couple of hours at home together, before driving off to Café Yazmina.

It was dark and cold as we trudged along Holloway Road and up the steps of the café. It felt awful knowing Flynn was so close. His family's flat was just a little further along this same road. I was still desperately hoping there'd be some way I could run away and see him one last time – but with Mum at my side, time was running out.

Inside, Café Yazmina was comfortingly familiar. The walls were painted pale blue and decorated with mosaic squares, many of which were chipped or cracked. The tables and chairs were simple – each one set with a tiny vase of flowers – and the dim orangey lights of the wall lamps gave off a soft glow.

I watched Mum look around. In contrast to the dirty, noisy road outside, the café was warm and inviting – though fairly empty as it was only six-thirty on a Monday evening. Some Turkish music was playing in the background and the air was lightly scented, the smell of herbs wafting in from the kitchen. I knew Mum would like all this. On the other hand, there was nothing swanky about the place at all – just basic cutlery to go with the simple tables and chairs. No linen tablecloths. No cloth napkins.

Yazmina herself bustled out to meet us. 'River.' She beamed at me, her dark eyes crinkling in the soft light. 'And you must be River's beautiful mother.' Yazmina swept up her long, tasselled skirt and did a sort of half-nod, half-bob in Mum's direction. 'Surely far too young for such a grown-up daughter?' She wound her thick dark hair round her silver-ringed fingers and smiled seductively.

For a minute she reminded me of Emmi – only about five times her size. Then she flung her arm out, indicating one of the waitresses in the corner. 'You see we are very demure here.' She pointed to the girl's black skirt and white shirt. 'Nothing to encourage the young men.' She flashed another pearly smile at Mum and raised her eyebrows. 'Let us sit.'

Mum looked a little taken aback but said nothing. I fingered the silver heart bracelet that Flynn had given me, as Yazmina sailed over to the nearest table and pulled out a chair for Mum. I slid into the one next to her. How on earth was I going to get away from Mum and slip along to Flynn's flat?

'Let me fetch some food . . . some refreshments . . .' Yazmina said.

'No. No. There's no need, Mrs . . . er . . .' Mum said, clearly embarrassed.

'Call me Yazmina. And of course there is a need.' Yazmina's eyes twinkled. 'I have prepared a little meal to show to you the sort of food we serve here. No greasy egg and chips, eh?' She chuckled.

'Well, that's very kind, but . . .' Mum sounded flustered. 'But we already have dinner plans.'

161

Yazmina waved her chubby arm and her silver bangles tinkled. 'This is only a small snack.' She leaned forwards. 'And an opportunity for us to talk.' She glanced at me, then back to Mum. 'Talk privately.' She winked.

I frowned. What on earth was there that Yazmina needed to talk to Mum privately about? For a second I felt vaguely insulted.

'Now, River, you know already the wages and the hours,' Yazmina said. 'Please go with Laila.' She pointed to the waitress in the corner. 'She will show you around the kitchen, and the ladies' toilet and little changing room, then take you upstairs to find a suitable skirt and blouse from my stores. 'She turned to Mum again. 'It's amazing how many staff over the years forget their work clothes. And they do get soiled. I would hate for River to ruin her own lovely clothes.'

'Well.' Mum still looked flustered. 'Er . . . that's very kind of you.'

I frowned. Why did I need to be shown the kitchen or the toilets? I'd been here plenty of times with Flynn already. And I was certainly capable of coming up with a black skirt and a white top on my own.

Yazmina's fleshy hand pressed down on my arm. 'Go on, River.' She gave my arm a squeeze. 'Go on.'

Slightly disgruntled, I let Laila lead me off into the kitchen. The two male chefs looked up from the hob in the far corner. They glanced at me then peered into their saucepans again, muttering to each other in Turkish. I looked around the kitchen. It was small but clean, with cupboards along one wall and a long stainless steel work surface near the door that led through to the storeroom.

'Wait here a sec,' Laila said.

I wandered across the room and leaned against the cupboards. I was wondering so deeply how on earth I was going to get away to see Flynn, that when I heard his voice behind me, I thought for one second the sound was in my head.

'Hey.' His hand touched my shoulder.

I gasped.

'Sssh.'

I spun round. He was standing right in front of me, his bruises faded, his eyes soft and tender. He leaned his face close in and whispered.

'Follow me.'

He took me through the door that led to the storeroom. But instead of going to the end of the corridor, he turned left and beckoned me up a narrow staircase. We emerged onto a little landing. I followed Flynn into a cosy living room. A long, low chaise longue covered with throws dominated the middle of the room. An exotically patterned rug was set in front of it. Tiny candles glowed on every surface.

'Oh.' I looked around, my eyes adjusting to the soft light. 'This is beautiful. Is it . . . ?'

'Yazmina's flat.' Flynn nodded. 'She said I could bring you up here. She's going to keep your mum talking. We've got twenty minutes.' He smiled and put his hands on my arms. 'So, how're you doing?'

I was still looking around, taking in the dark wooden furniture and the thick silk wall hangings in deep reds and blues. Everything seemed to flicker in the candlelight.

'The candles are so pretty,' I said.

'They were my idea.' Flynn flushed slightly. 'I wanted it to be special . . .'

I stared at him. He was smiling but his face was strained. Anxious.

'I wanted to make it so special that nothing and no one else will ever be better,' he said hesitantly. 'I don't want you to find someone else.'

'I won't.' I stood there, staring steadily at him. 'No one will ever be better because there will never be anyone else. Ever.'

'Oh, Riv.' Flynn hugged me then pulled away, drawing me down to the sofa to sit beside him.

'You'll have guys after you all the time. Look at you.' He sighed. 'Listen. I'm going to call whenever I can. And as soon as I get a job in Dublin I'm saving up to come back and visit you. I don't care about anything else. And you'll save up too, won't you? Yazmina pays okay and you'll get tips here as well.'

I nodded.

Flynn checked the clock over the fireplace. 'Fifteen minutes.' He lay back on the sofa and raised his eyebrows. 'Now, what can we do with our last fifteen minutes?'

I rolled my eyes, expecting him to pull me into a kiss, maybe even take things further. But Flynn just lay there, gazing up at me.

I frowned. 'Are you seriously asking?'

He nodded. 'I told you. I want this to be special. We can talk or whatever you want.' He reached and touched the little heart on my silver bracelet. Then he ran the back of his hand down the inside of my arm. 'You are the most beautiful person I've ever met,' he whispered. 'Beautiful inside and out.'

A lump came into my throat. I lay down beside him. 'Really?' I forced a grin onto my face. 'Stone says my eyes are the colour of ditchwater.'

Flynn snorted. 'Someone needs to find Stone a

165

freakin' girlfriend.' He rested his hand in the dip of my waist. 'I hope you're impressed by how restrained I'm being here,' he grinned. 'Because it's killing me not kissing you.'

I laughed. But the lump in my throat was lodged so firmly that it hurt. 'Maybe I'd rather have a poem than a kiss,' I said, remembering one of the first conversations Flynn and I ever had.

'Whoa.' Flynn chuckled. 'Okay then. Roses are red, violets are blue. River, you're mad, but I still love you.'

I grinned. 'That was rubbish.'

Flynn's eyes widened. 'Oh, really? Okay, Miss Only-Posh-Poems-Will-Do.' He paused. 'How about: *Can I go forward when my heart is here?*'

'That's not a proper poem. Plus it isn't even original. That's from *Romeo and Juliet*.'

Flynn gazed at me. I was expecting him to come back at me with some clever, witty remark, but he didn't. He just kept on gazing at me.

'It's how it is though, isn't it?' he said.

The lump in my throat hardened. I stared at his face – at the strong lines of it and the sad eyes. How could I be losing that face?

'Listen,' Flynn said. 'About my da. I don't think he'll come up to you once he knows we've gone. He'll probably just assume we've split up or something, so I doubt he'll think he can get any money off you.'

'I'm sure he won't.'

'Okay, but if he does turn up, please just walk away. And tell your mum. Tell James. He's promised me he'll look out for you and . . .'

'I'll never love anyone as much as I love you, right at this moment,' I said.

Flynn closed his eyes, his lips trembling slightly. Then he looked across at the clock above the little fireplace opposite the sofa. 'Eleven minutes left,' he said. 'It's not enough time for anything.'

'I think we both know that's not true.' I tried to laugh, but it was no good. The time for being all dry and ironic was over. The weight in my chest was going to suffocate me. I couldn't even cry and wash it away.

'Flynn?' My voice cracked.

'What would you like now?' Flynn's eyes gleamed miserably in the candlelight. 'Another poem?'

I shook my head and moved closer. 'I've changed my mind,' I said. 'I'd rather have a kiss.'

Ten minutes later we were back downstairs. We didn't say anything as we stood in the corridor outside the kitchen. I clung to Flynn, feeling numb. This wasn't really happening, was it? Surely I would see him as usual tomorrow or the next day?

'Just a bit longer?' I pleaded.

Flynn shook his head, pushing me gently away. 'We can't risk your mum finding me here. She'll take it out on you – stop you working here.'

'Okay.' I drew back and stared at his face – trying to imprint it on my brain. It swam, blurrily, in front of my eyes. He bent down and kissed me. Then he pushed open the door and stood back. I hesitated for a second then stumbled into the kitchen. I heard the door swing shut behind me. I didn't look back.

I crossed the room to the other door – the one that led back into the café. Laila materialised beside me. She shoved a plastic bag into my hands. 'Your skirt and blouse,' she said with a smile.

I stared at her blankly, then wiped my face, took a deep breath and pushed the door open. The café had filled up since I'd been gone and there was a real buzz about the place. Honey and cardamom scents wafted towards me from a nearby table, mingling with the clatter of knives and forks and the hum of good-humoured conversation. Mum and Yazmina were still sitting across the room. Mum's fork was poised above her plate and she was chatting animatedly. She looked up and saw me.

'River?' she smiled. 'Did you get your outfit? I was thinking of sending a search party.'

I stared at her stupidly. Outfit? Then I felt the handle of the plastic bag sweating into my hand. Oh yes. I nodded then stretched a smile across my lips.

'Yes, thanks, Yazmina.'

Yazmina caught my eye and winked. I nodded, acknowledging that I was really thanking her for those last few minutes with Flynn.

'Have you had a nice meal, Mum?' I asked.

'Oh yes, Yazmina's been telling me about how she set up the café. And the food here is delicious.'

I wanted to smile for real now. Yazmina had clearly done an unbelievable charm job on Mum. But my eyes felt dull and heavy.

'Are you all right, River?' Mum frowned. 'You *were* gone a long time.'

Yazmina rose up from the table and billowed her way towards me. She put her arm round me and gave my shoulder a meaningful squeeze. 'Even for a simple white blouse and black skirt a girl must make sure the fit is correct and the style flattering,' she said. 'Yes, River?'

I nodded and smiled. 'Yes.' I felt nothing. Nothing at all. Just an agonising weight in my chest.

Mum checked her watch. 'We have to go, River. Stone will be back from football soon and expecting some tea.'

'Right.'

I followed Mum down the steps of the café. I wondered if Flynn was watching me from Yazmina's living room. I looked up, but I couldn't see him.

Mum's heels click-clacked towards her car. As the lights flashed, telling us the doors were open, this scream started up inside my head. No words, just a long, thin, silent scream. We were going. We were leaving and Flynn was there. He was still inside. He was so close. It wasn't too late. I could go back in, I could beg him to stay . . .

But if I went back in now, Mum would know Flynn was there. And it wouldn't do any good anyway. We'd still have to say goodbye. This was it.

I got into the car and let Mum drive me away.

She chattered on, asking to see my uniform. I shook out a mid-length skirt and a soft, pretty white top from the bag. They looked as if they'd fit me perfectly. Mum glanced sideways and nodded.

'Yazmina seems very nice,' she said approvingly. 'And very caring to the girls who work there. She told me about her life growing up in Turkey. Fascinating past. She's divorced too, you know.' She patted my knee. 'I think this job will be a great thing for you. Just the thing to keep you busy.'

I glanced at her. *Just the thing to help me get over Flynn.* That was what she meant. I looked back at

170

the café, tuning Mum out. Listening to the long scream in my head.

It isn't over. It won't ever be over.

I don't ever want to get over him.

19

The first week was bad. I stumbled from school to home – experiencing the world as though everything was wrapped in cotton wool and I couldn't quite touch it. As if *I* were wrapped in cotton wool and it couldn't touch *me*. The heavy weight didn't shift from my chest, though I learned to live around it – eating enough food to fuel my body and concentrating sufficiently in class to avoid being picked on for not paying attention.

The second week was worse. The numb, cotton-wool feeling started to wear off. And the thin scream that had started in my head as I'd walked away from the café became this permanent background noise to my life. Wherever I was, whatever I was doing, inside my head I was screaming. It was the rawest, unhappiest feeling I'd ever known. Flynn and I messaged and spoke whenever we could. But it didn't stop me missing him so much that I felt like I was going mad with it.

Maybe we were trying not to upset each other, but we shied away from talking about how we felt most of the time. Flynn told me about Ireland, about his family and how they were settling in, and what his new sixth form college was like. He mentioned there were girls in his class. Twice. I tried not to let my jealousy about this show. I didn't want him to keep things from me and I didn't want to make him angry. I was scared of having an argument with him and there being no way of properly making up.

Emmi and Grace tried to help me in their different ways. As soon as I was no longer grounded they kept asking me to go out with them after school and at weekends. Emmi took me shopping and told me how fabulous I looked in everything I tried on. Grace let me use her phone to call Flynn a few times. It was very generous of her but it wasn't enough.

I was hoping that in another week or so Mum would stop checking my phone account, but so far she showed no sign of letting up.

Emmi and Grace knew I was missing Flynn. But in spite of our friendship I didn't tell them just how badly I was hurting. Partly because I knew that neither of them really liked Flynn. But mostly because I didn't know how to explain what I was feeling. All I knew was that I was sinking and screaming into some dark place where no one could reach me.

For the first couple of weeks they accepted it when I said I didn't want to go out, but after that they started pushing me to do things with them. So I threw myself into my GCSEs, explaining I'd hardly done any work for the last two months, and had loads to catch up on with the exams just a few months away. Emmi was particularly dismissive of this as an excuse but Mum, of course, loved it.

I was hiding how I felt from Mum as much as from my friends. Luckily, she was used to us not talking much anymore, so I guess it didn't seem odd to her that I spent so much time alone. Working hard was a good reason for staying in. And I did work hard. Essays and reading and writing were places where I could lose myself for a few minutes – the only Flynn-free time I ever got, apart from when things got busy at the café, and I was dashing about, sweat beading on my forehead, taking orders and serving food.

I liked working at the café. Yazmina always asked after Flynn. She told me on my first evening how he'd begged her to let her use the upstairs room 'to say goodbye to his lovely girl'. She beamed. 'I thought this was so romantic, how could I say no? And then he ask me to keep your mother out of the way. Which is perhaps not so romantic. But he smiles at me and I cannot say no. He is charm, that boy. When he wants. Charm. You know?'

I knew.

Two more weeks passed. I still thought about Flynn all the time. His voice. His face. His touch.

That was all that was real. Everything else was just passing by at a distance. I lived for the moments when I spoke to him and I spent almost all the rest of my time wrapped up in my head, hurting.

This has to pass, I thought.

Soon, this has to pass.

February got warmer. It was ironic, I thought, that Flynn and I had only gone out together during the depths of winter, when it had been difficult to find places where we didn't freeze. And now the weather was mild and we could have spent whole days in the park. And instead he was in Ireland, where he told me glumly it hadn't stopped raining for weeks. And I was here, looking at the sunshine flooding through my window, wishing I was out in it with Flynn.

It was a month to the day when Flynn had left. I was walking home from school not thinking about anything in particular, just experiencing the usual dull ache in my chest. I heard heavy footsteps right behind me and looked over my shoulder. Flynn's dad padded up.

'Hello there,' he smiled.

I blinked. He looked almost exactly like that first time I'd seen him in the hair salon, except there was a small scar across his nose – presumably from where Flynn had hit him – and his hands weren't shaking.

'Hi,' I said uncertainly. Flynn had made me promise to walk away without a word if his da showed up. But it wasn't so easy. How could I just ignore the man? He was standing right in front of me.

'So Patrick and the others have gone,' he said. He was still smiling. I relaxed a little. He didn't seem drunk, he wasn't slurring his words or staggering about like he had in the church.

I nodded.

'That was a bad business, eh?' Flynn's dad scratched his nose. 'I could've pressed charges, you know.'

I nodded again. There was an awkward silence.

'Are you . . . all right now?' I stammered, feeling embarrassed.

Flynn's dad sighed. 'I'm fine, though it's been difficult to work, of course.'

I stared at him.

'Been off for weeks, I have,' he said pointedly. 'Hard to make ends meet. Very hard.' He looked away for a second, then back at me – his eyes full of appeal in an expression exactly like one of Flynn's.

Oh my goodness. He was asking me for money.

'My mum stopped giving me any cash,' I said. 'She was angry with me . . .' I tailed off, not wanting to give more away.

Flynn's dad raised his eyebrows. 'That's ironic, eh?' he said. 'Wherever Patrick goes, there's a lot of anger.'

I wanted to say something in Flynn's defence, but I couldn't think what. I gulped. More than anything I just wanted to get away from his dad.

'I'm sorry,' I said. I fished in my pocket and drew out a five-pence piece. 'See, that's all I have,' I said.

To my surprise, Flynn's dad reached out and took the coin. Then he hesitated for a second and put it back in my palm. 'Oh well,' he said. 'Sorry to have troubled you.' He turned and shuffled off.

I didn't tell Flynn when I next spoke to him. I'd intended to, but when the time came I couldn't bring myself. I knew Flynn would be angry – angry with his dad for pestering me and angry with me for not walking away immediately, like I'd promised I would.

It was getting harder to talk to him anyway. Like our present lives weren't connected anymore. I didn't know the people he talked about. His new friends. And he was out of touch with everyone at home except for James. I knew they still messaged on Facebook most days. James occasionally mentioned him when we were out as well, but not often.

Sometimes it felt like Flynn only really existed in my head.

Half-term started at the very end of February. On Saturday I went to a party. Emmi had been nagging me to come out with her and Alex for weeks now. I'd avoided Alex as much as possible since he'd accused Flynn of stealing his iPad, but I knew his parents had bought a new model for him with the insurance and nobody had mentioned the subject for ages.

Anyway, what did it really matter now?

Getting ready to go out with Grace and Emmi was fun. I even found myself laughing . . . looking forward to the evening. Practically everyone from our year was going to be there and I was borrowing one of Emmi's more restrained tops, a silky, sleeveless blue number, which both the others said I looked gorgeous in.

Alex turned up with a load of mates – several of whom I recognised from his and Flynn's school. Emmi flitted around reintroducing me, clearly hoping to set me up with one of them. I got hit on a bit, but I didn't say much in return and all the boys eventually gave up and moved on to other girls who smiled back at them and spoke in more than uninterested grunts.

As the evening went on, the fun started to fade. Everyone was either busy getting off their faces or getting together. Grace and James were chatting happily. Emmi was surrounded by adoring boys. And Alex, who'd barely nodded a 'hello' at me, was showing off in some drinking game with his mates.

I sat on the staircase, watching everyone, feeling more lonely than ever.

And then my phone rang. I didn't hear it at first, over the party noise, but I picked it up after a few rings and squinted at the number.

It was Flynn. He didn't normally call me on my phone – thanks to Mum's obsessive checking of my call log.

I snatched the phone to my ear. 'Hello?'

'Hello, beautiful.' Flynn's strong, expressive voice sent a thrill of joy through me.

'Hi,' I said, grinning from ear to ear.

'How are you?' he said.

'Fine.' It was hard to hear him, thanks to the music next door. I stuck my finger in my ear to shut out the sound. 'Bored, actually. I'm at this party and —'

'A party?' Flynn laughed, but there was a hollow sound to his voice.

'Yeah,' I said. 'Emmi made me come.'

'Is Alex there too?' Flynn said.

'Of course,' I said. 'He's her boyfriend and it's his mate's party.'

I stopped talking, worrying that Flynn might see me going to the same party as Alex as disloyal, after all the accusations Alex had made.

'I'm not here because of Emmi and Alex,' I went on. 'It's just something to do.'

There was a long pause. All I could hear on the other end of the phone was Flynn's shallow breathing.

'Right,' he snapped. 'Well, I hope you all have a lovely time together.'

'That's not fair,' I said, hurt by his harsh tone.

'I tell you what's not fair, River,' Flynn spat. 'You being there and me being here without you.'

He sounded furious, like he was angry with *me* about it. Looking back, I guess he was just feeling miserable but, at the time, when I felt so lonely already, it was too much to take.

'Well, whose fault's that?' I snapped, irritation bubbling up inside me. 'If you could keep a lid on your temper, maybe you wouldn't have forced your entire family to move abroad.'

'Okay, well it's good to know what you really think.' Flynn's voice was low and sarcastic. 'Bye.'

The line went dead. I stared at the phone. Flynn had hung up on me.

The shock of it winded me for a second then searing misery rolled up from my gut. This was what I'd been afraid of happening . . . an argument – with no way of making up properly.

I sat, too stunned even to cry for a couple of minutes, then I forced myself to get up and go back to the party. Everyone was still having a great time. I felt worse than ever. Part of me wanted to call Flynn back but *I* wasn't the one who'd hung up. Why should I make the first move?

I waited an hour. He didn't call. My misery faded and I got angrier and angrier with him. I rang Mum and asked her to come and pick me up. I was dreading her checking my call log – but she was in a good mood and didn't bother.

I got home just after midnight and crept up to my room, still feeling furious. I went to bed and – eventually – to sleep. But Flynn still didn't call.

* * *

I slept late and woke when Dad rang on our front door bell. He had come to take me and Stone to the commune for a few days. I checked my phone straight away. Nothing from Flynn.

I had to speak to him before the long car journey up to the commune. Ignoring the angry, upset voice in my head which said he should be calling me, I rang him, but his phone was switched off.

Now I felt really furious. How *dare* Flynn not call me? How *dare* he not answer?

Dad put his head round my bedroom door and said we needed to leave – he wanted to get back to the commune as soon as possible.

'Fine,' I said. 'I'll be down in a sec.'

I sat on my bed and tried Flynn again. Nothing. I felt sick. Flynn was angry with me – and all over nothing. Tears leaked out of my eyes. I had to reach him. I *had* to. Panic swirled in my chest. I could call again and leave a message – or send a text. A text seemed easiest. My thumb hovered over the keypad, as I wondered what to write. An apology? An explanation?

As I started writing that I was sorry, the fear vanished and fury rose up inside me again. This was ridiculous. *Flynn* was being ridiculous. I mean, why should *I* be sorry? I hadn't done anything wrong. I wasn't the one who'd hung up. Flynn hadn't even bothered to call me. He was probably still sure he was right, and angry with me – that's if he was thinking about me at all.

I switched off my mobile. Let's see how he liked not being able to get hold of me.

I shoved the phone under my mattress, picked up my bag and stormed downstairs to where Dad was waiting.

20

We arrived at the commune just after midday. Dad explained that Gemma hadn't been well recently – the same problem, he said, that had made her ill and prevented him from visiting us a few weeks ago. I got the strong sense that there was something important he wasn't telling us, but he kept saying it was nothing to worry about and, to be honest, my mind was still all on Flynn. I was starting to regret having left my phone behind. Not that I wanted to call him – but I didn't have anyone's numbers stored anywhere else, so I couldn't speak to any of my friends, either.

Gemma was sitting outside in the sunshine, waiting for us. She and Dad had a quiet word then Dad made some sandwiches and took me and Stone off for a long walk. Stone grumbled about it but I was quite happy to be outside. Dad's at his best in the open air – and, unlike practically everyone else in my life, he never pushes me to talk about stuff when I'm not ready.

By the time we got back, I'd resigned myself to not having my phone. It was only for four more days. And maybe time away from the rest of my life would be good.

I had a bath, then it was time for the big dinner they had in the communal kitchen every night. Residents took it in turns to cook. There were usually lots of people around, but the commune was fairly quiet at the moment. One family had just moved out, while John and Julia were away, leaving just the nerdy computer guy and Ros – my favourite member of the commune – an outspoken, ex-actress friend of Gemma's who was great fun except when she started talking about feminist politics.

Ros and Gemma had made a huge veggie lasagne. Normally I love Gemma's food. But today it tasted like mucus and cardboard. I ate a couple of mouthfuls then told Dad I had a headache. I went up to Dad and Gemma's apartment. I was sleeping in the small room – kind of a storeroom with a camp bed in it. Dad and Gemma also had a private living room – with a sofa bed where Stone was sleeping – and their own bedroom and bathroom. That's how commune accommodation works – everyone gets a few private rooms but is expected to cook and eat with the group.

I curled up on the bed. The room was dark and cold, but I couldn't be bothered to get undressed. In the end I had to pee. When I came back I crawled under the covers and lay there, feeling numb.

Eventually, footsteps outside told me Dad and Gemma were coming to bed. There was a soft rap on my door then it creaked open. I lay still, eyes tight shut, trying to make my breathing slow and even. The door shut again and the footsteps padded away. I opened my eyes and stared into the darkness – always deeper at the commune than at home – then buried myself further under the covers.

It was a long time before I fell asleep.

When I woke up, the sun was shining. It was a beautiful day. Dad and Gemma were out in the field below my window, wandering hand in hand down to the trees that formed a barrier with the road. I felt better for my long sleep. Somehow it was comforting knowing that Flynn couldn't reach me, even if he wanted to.

I worked outside all morning with Ros. She didn't mention Flynn or ask me any awkward questions, but she made me laugh with her tales and jokes about her ex-boyfriends. Later, I worked on my GCSEs – forcing myself for some masochistic reason to make a real effort with the subjects I most hated – maths and science.

The next day I spent the whole time outside with Dad. There was always lots to do in the commune – planting and weeding and stuff. I'd lost interest in it a couple of years ago but right now it was just what I needed. I could tell Dad was pleased I was joining in.

Late afternoon on my second day I was helping Dad mend the hen hutch. I didn't much like the hens – the scratchy way they walked and their beady eyes. So I looked away, towards the sky, turning round only to hand Dad nails and bits of wood when he asked for them.

Dad's a silent kind of guy. He had his shirt sleeves rolled up and was concentrating hard on what he was doing, his tongue just peeking out from between his lips. So I had plenty of time to think. I tried to focus on the English essay I was planning to write the next day. But my mind kept drifting off towards Flynn.

What was he doing right now? Had he tried to call me yet? How did he feel about my phone being switched off?

'River?' Dad's voice filtered through my thoughts. 'River?'

'Mmmn?' I squinted towards his silhouette. The

sun was shining high and bright in the sky behind
him.

'I asked you to pass me one of the long nails,' Dad
said calmly.

'Right.' I turned round and rummaged in the tool-
box at my feet. A shadow fell over the ground
around me as I picked out a five-inch nail.

Dad was standing over me, blocking the sunlight.
I handed him the nail.

'Thanks.' He carried on standing there for a moment
then cleared his throat. 'River, I didn't want to load
you down with this because I know you've been
through a lot, recently.' He hesitated, squinting at me.

I smiled, registering how rough and weatherbeaten his skin looked. 'Spit it out, Dad,' I said.

'Okay, well . . .' Dad rubbed his forehead. 'When I
said Gemma was ill, what I meant was that she'd
had a miscarriage . . .'

'Really?' I stared at him, shocked. I hadn't expected
that. 'She was *pregnant*?'

Dad sighed. 'Yes, we had a scare a while back
which is why we didn't say she was pregnant before
and why I couldn't see you a few weeks ago and, I
suppose, why I haven't been as focused as I should
have been on you.' He paused. 'She finally lost the
baby about ten days ago.'

'Is she okay?' I said.

'Gemma's fine, love,' Dad said. 'The baby was very small and there's no problem with Gemma having more.'

'*More?*' I looked at him over the hutch, suddenly feeling all churned up. 'Do you . . . want more?'

Dad met my gaze. 'The baby wasn't planned, but it would have been very much loved.' He paused. 'If it was just me then, no, I probably wouldn't choose to have more children. You and Stone are everything to me. But Gemma doesn't have kids of her own. It's natural she wants to be a mother.'

I nodded. I didn't know what to think. It seemed selfish to object. After all, I wasn't a little kid myself anymore. Anyway, a baby would be cool.

'Was . . . was it a girl or a boy?' I asked.

'A girl.' Dad looked sad.

A girl. She would have been my little sister. Like Caitlin was to Flynn. My mind filled with all the things we could have done. I might have dressed her up and taken her out. I could have taught her to swim and do her hair in different styles and held her hand when she got scared in the night or at the movies. But now . . . my eyes brimmed with tears.

'Poor Gemma,' I said. 'Poor you, Dad.'

Dad walked around the hutch and gave me a hug.

I tilted my face to the sun, letting it warm my face. Then Dad drew back.

'Part of me didn't want to tell you . . . didn't want to share all the hurt that we feel. Then I realised you're almost an adult and that's what grown-ups who love each other do: share our pain with those who care about us.' He paused. 'So . . . do you still miss Flynn?'

I froze, pulling away. Dad hadn't mentioned Flynn since we arrived. I'd kind of assumed he thought I was over him.

'What makes you think that?' I asked, my face burning.

'Because I have eyes,' Dad said.

I stared at him. Normally he was dead laid-back. If I didn't answer him he'd assume I didn't want to talk and leave me alone. But right now he was actually frowning at me, his bright blue eyes narrowed.

'Please, River,' he said. 'If you're hurting, I'd like to help.'

'I don't want to talk about it,' I muttered.

'Well I do.' Dad put his hands on his hips. 'I'm worried about you. Gemma said she thought she heard you crying last night.'

'That was nothing.' My lips trembled.

Dad's face crumpled with sympathy. 'Riv, I hate to

see you so unhappy.' He paused. 'Has Flynn been in touch with you? Please talk to me.'

I looked down. A long nail lay at my feet, glinting in the sun. I couldn't see the point of talking to Dad about Flynn. I mean, what would I say? That I missed him? The words hardly covered how deeply I felt – how my heart felt like it had been ripped out of my chest. Anyway, how could Dad understand?

'I'm sorry, River,' Dad said slowly. 'It must be very hard . . . missing him.'

I still said nothing.

Dad sighed. 'You know, rage like he showed – with no boundaries – that's a scary reality. Short of some kind of spiritual turnaround or a lot of hard work in therapy – well, it's difficult for people to change . . .'

I looked away.

Dad sighed again. 'Okay,' he said. 'Okay.' He squatted down by the hen hutch and we carried on with our mending. Gemma came out with some water for us a few minutes later. I gave her a big hug, not knowing how to tell her I was sorry about the baby. I think she understood. She said thank you as she gave me a big squeeze back. I sat, resting against the hutch, and watched as she talked quietly with Dad about some shopping that was needed.

I picked up the long nail I'd noticed on the ground earlier and rolled it over my palm. The metal was warm in my hand. How could Dad possibly know what I was going through? He was so settled in his life with Gemma. Plus, for all his concern, he had still stood right beside Mum and agreed I shouldn't see Flynn anymore.

I shoved the nail into the earth at my feet and turned back to the hen hutch.

Two days later Dad drove us home.

I went straight upstairs, retrieved my phone and switched it on. My heart stopped as I scanned the voicemails and texts. At least six from Flynn, plus several from Emmi and Grace.

I played Flynn's calls – a series of increasingly desperate messages, ending with him asking if I was dumping him:

'. . . and please listen, I love you and I'm so sorry and please call me . . .'

My heart hammered as I sat on the edge of the bed and rang Flynn's number. The mobile was out of range. *No.* My heart sank. I couldn't even leave him a message. Before I had time to think about it too much I punched in a text: *Been away. No phone. Back now. Call me.* I hesitated then added: *I love you.*

I pressed 'send'. There. It was done.

I went back downstairs to say goodbye to Dad. Mum was full of how healthy I looked from all my time spent outdoors at the commune.

'And River did loads of GCSE work,' Dad said proudly. 'She's really turned things around, you know.'

Mum sniffed, but I could tell she was pleased.

I clutched the phone in my pocket. How could my parents be so unaware of what I was going through? I suddenly felt horribly alone. I said goodbye to Dad and slunk off back upstairs. I tried Flynn several more times, but his phone stayed out of range.

I slept badly all night, drifting in and out of anxiety-fuelled dreams. I woke up late, all bleary, to the sound of my mobile ringing.

I seized it up from beside the bed before I was even properly awake. 'Hello?'

'River? Thank God.' His voice broke as he spoke.

'Oh Flynn.' I burst into tears. Maybe it was the relief of speaking to him at last. Maybe it was all the stress of the past few days. Maybe it was just the sound of his voice.

'I'm so sorry I got so cross,' Flynn said. 'When I thought about it, I realised you had every right to go to any stupid party you wanted to. I tried to get hold of you the next day, but you didn't answer . . .'

'I . . . I was at my dad's commune,' I sniffed. 'I left my phone at home.'

'I missed you so much.' Flynn's voice sounded miserable and heavy. He sighed. 'This is so awful, River. Being apart like this.'

'I know.' I sat up in bed, wiping the tears off my face. 'So where were you last night?' I said. 'How come you were out of range?'

'Just out,' he said. 'Nothing special.'

I frowned. There was something guarded about his voice. Flynn was such a good actor it was hard to be sure, but I sensed there was something he wasn't telling me.

'Out where?' I said.

'Just out. With a few mates. Some stupid thing . . . It doesn't matter.'

'What happened?'

A long silence.

'I just . . . did something stupid,' Flynn stammered.

'What kind of stupid?'

'Nothing that affects us,' he insisted. 'Look, it doesn't matter, Riv, all that matters is that we're okay and I've got a job and I'm going to save my money and we'll see each other soon, yeah?'

'Okay.' I smiled at the earnestness in his voice but, a few minutes later, I came off the phone feeling troubled. There was something Flynn was keeping from me about what he'd been up to. What was the 'stupid' thing he'd done? Had he got into another fight? Was it something to do with another girl?

I called Emmi and she invited me round on Saturday night. Her parents were away and she, Alex and a few other friends were hanging out in their house. I made out I had to go to a family party with Mum and said I'd see her at school on Monday. I couldn't face Emmi and Alex and their loud, show-off friends. I didn't belong with those people. I didn't belong here at all.

I only belonged with Flynn.

And that's when I decided: I was going to go to Ireland and see Flynn. I'd already saved quite a lot from my job at Café Yazmina. To make up enough to pay for my ticket, I'd pretend I needed money for a school trip, maybe forge a letter from school to convince Mum. However I did it, I was going to get myself to Ireland and see Flynn, face to face. I sat there all evening, planning it out. I even started on the fake school letter, sneaking into Mum's files to find an old one I could use to scan the letterhead. Once I had the cash in my hand, I would simply tell Mum I was spending the weekend with Dad. Then I'd just leave. By the time they realised I wasn't with either of them, I'd already be on the plane.

Yes.

Suddenly the whole world seemed brighter. I went to bed on Sunday night not even minding about going back to school the next day.

And then, on Monday morning, the bombshell dropped.

21

'What's the matter with Grace?' Emmi whispered.

We were in the middle of our first lesson – English. Emmi had spent ten minutes before class telling me again that I'd missed a great night with her, Alex and their friends on Saturday. We'd noticed that Grace hadn't shown up for registration and assumed she was probably just a bit late. But now, as I followed Emmi's pointing finger, it was clear something was very wrong.

Grace was standing in the doorway, ashen-faced. Mrs Bunton waved her impatiently to her seat. Grace's cheeks remained pale as she crept past everyone towards her desk. That, in itself, was odd. Grace normally went red if someone asked her what the time was, let alone if she had to cross a crowded classroom with everyone staring at her. I peered more closely. Was she wearing really heavy make-up? Grace drew nearer, her head bowed. *Jeez*, she was. Masses of foundation, then loads of black eyeliner. She looked like a different person. She glanced at me as she took her seat. *Whoa*. Close to it was obvious that she had been crying. Her eyes were red-rimmed and bloodshot. Was the make-up an attempt to disguise that?

I raised my eyebrows at her. 'What's the matter?' I mouthed.

Grace shook her head and bent over her bag. She didn't look up again.

After English she rushed off to her next class without speaking to either me or Emmi.

'Where's she going?' I said.

'Geography,' Emmi said. 'I've got it too. I'll find out what's going on. See you lunchtime, yeah?'

I nodded, wondering what the matter could be. From the state Grace was in it looked serious. I couldn't believe it was anything to do with James. I couldn't imagine him either dumping her or cheating on her. Maybe it was something at home, something to do with her parents.

It niggled away at me throughout the rest of the morning. I felt guilty as well as worried. Grace had been so generous recently, letting me borrow her phone to call Flynn when Mum was still checking my call log. How was it possible that I had no idea what was upsetting her now? The more I considered it, the more I realised how selfish I'd been. So wrapped up in my own problems I hadn't thought about anyone else.

As soon as the bell rang for break I went to look for Grace. She was probably still with Emmi, but they weren't in any of the places I'd have expected: not the cafeteria nor the patch of garden outside the gym nor our form room. I checked out the toilets on every floor too. There was no sign of them – and both their phones were switched off.

I wandered around the school, hoping I'd bump into them. I tried the cafeteria one last time then headed across the playground.

There. I saw them in the distance. Even before I could hear them it was obvious they were arguing. Emmi was poking her finger in Grace's face and Grace was weeping and gesticulating with her hands.

As I got closer I caught Emmi saying, 'Of course you can. You *have* to.'

'I can't,' Grace wailed.

They didn't notice me until I was just a few metres away. As they turned in my direction it was obvious Grace had been crying again. Her black eye make-up was in streaks down her face.

Both of them looked embarrassed at having been seen.

'What's going on?' I said uncertainly.

Emmi looked across at Grace.

'No,' Grace hissed.

'Are you all right?' I said, feeling all my old insecurities twisting in my stomach. What was going on? Why didn't Grace want to talk to me? Why was it okay for her to talk to Emmi but not to me?

Emmi shuffled impatiently. 'James did something she's annoyed about so . . .'

'Not *here*,' Grace hissed again.

The bell rang.

Grace grabbed Emmi by the wrist and started dragging her towards the school building. 'Hurry up, you need to help me with my make-up before I'm late for something else.'

As Emmi let Grace pull her away, she looked over her shoulder.

'My place after school, Riv? Okay?' she said.

I nodded, feeling confused. The sun came out as I walked across the playground. It sounded like Grace was upset over something James had done, but maybe Emmi was making that up to stop me from guessing what the real problem was.

Was it something to do with my friendship with Emmi and Grace? Neither of them much liked

Flynn. I'd refused to see Emmi on Saturday and I'd hardly talked to Grace about her life for weeks.

I felt desperately torn. On the one hand, when I imagined the moment I'd tell Flynn I was coming to see him, a warm glow spread through me. But, on the other hand, when I took a step back from my relationship, I could see how it was creating a big distance between me and my friends.

I drifted through French and then history, barely paying attention. As the bell rang for the end of the day I looked over at Grace again. She looked unbearably miserable. I felt another stab of guilt. She'd been so supportive, always, about me and Flynn. And recently – I felt ashamed to think it – I really hadn't been a very good friend to her.

Well, tonight I would be. If she was having problems with James, I would listen and do whatever I could to help.

Emmi sauntered over and raised her eyes at us both. 'Can we get out of here please?'

I called Mum and told her I was popping into Emmi's on my way home but that I wouldn't be late. Grace was very quiet all the way there. As we followed Emmi up the wide staircase to her huge bedroom I squeezed her hand, wondering what on earth James had done to make her so upset. She didn't look around.

We walked into Emmi's room. She slammed the door shut and flopped down on the bed. 'Right, Grace. Enough already. Tell River.'

'Tell me what?'

Grace looked at me anxiously.

'Go on,' Emmi said exasperatedly.

There was a long pause. 'I saw something on James's phone this morning when we walked to school together,' she stammered.

I stared at her, not seeing what she meant. Then I thought I understood. 'You mean . . . you mean pictures of girls?' I said.

Grace looked at Emmi's pale green carpet.

I glanced at Emmi. She was staring crossly at Grace.

'Is that why you're upset?' I said to Grace. 'Because . . . I know it's disgusting but it doesn't mean he doesn't care about *you*. Anyway, they all . . . Unless. Oh, Grace. It wasn't something really gross, was it?'

'Me and James had a huge row.' Grace's eyes welled with tears. 'I don't think he's talking to me now.'

'Oh, Grace, that's—' I started.

'For goodness sake, Grace,' Emmi snapped. 'Will you explain this properly, please?'

202

Grace didn't look up from the carpet. 'It was on Facebook,' she mumbled.

On Facebook? Now I was confused. You couldn't post anything all that outrageous on Facebook – the network wouldn't allow you to.

'What?' I said. 'I don't understand.'

'Look for yourself.' Emmi snatched up her laptop and pressed the keys.

I sat, waiting, feeling completely confused.

And then Emmi turned the computer towards me and I saw.

It was Flynn's Facebook page.

'Check out his latest status,' Emmi said, drily.

I looked more closely. There was a photo of Flynn, smiling, with his arm round a girl in a bikini, a fat wad of money in his hand. Underneath the picture it read: *another awesome result from the iPad bank !!!!*

I stared at the picture, my mind in free fall. 'When did this go up?' I asked.

'Early this morning,' Emmi said grimly, pointing to the date by the post.

I thought back to my conversation with Flynn yesterday. He'd said he'd done something stupid during the week . . . I'd imagined a fight . . . had he instead been out somewhere, posing for pictures with some bimbo and with more than enough money to pay for ten tickets home to see me?

I couldn't process it. It didn't make sense. If he knew he'd been stupid, why boast about it on his Facebook page where I was bound to see it? Or, if the boasting was the stupid thing he'd done, why not just delete the post?

'Why's he talking about an "iPad bank"?' I said 'What does that mean?'

Grace and Emmi exchanged glances.

'It's obviously a reference to all the money he's made selling stolen iPads,' Emmi said, drily.

'What?' I stared at her.

'He must be referring to Alex's iPad at the very least, don't you think?' Grace sniffed.

'But Flynn didn't take Alex's iPad,' I said, feeling completely bewildered.

'I think this proves he did.' Emmi snorted. 'And from the look of all that cash and the word "another", it looks like Alex wasn't the only person he stole from.'

'No way,' I said. 'I mean why would he boast about that?'

'He probably thinks nothing can touch him, now he's in Ireland,' Emmi said. 'Face it, River, he's a thug and a thief. He's obviously stolen *loads* of stuff.'

'James didn't think so,' Grace said.

I turned to her.

'What did James actually say?' My voice sounded hoarse to my ears. I felt numb.

Grace's eyes filled with tears again.

'This page was open on his phone so I asked him what it was and he said "nothing" and I asked him if he'd looked at the girl in the bikini and he said of course he had because he was looking at Flynn with all that money and wondering how he'd got it. And I asked him how long he'd looked at the girl and he said he hadn't been counting and I—'

'Shut up, Grace.' Emmi folded her arms. 'The bikini pic's the least of it. It's the fact that Flynn's boasting about his stupid "iPad bank".'

'But Flynn *wouldn't*,' I said, desperate for a different interpretation of what looked like proof Flynn had stolen stuff and lied to all of us. Lied to *me*. I turned to Grace. 'James didn't believe Flynn was a thief. You *said* so.'

'James would *always* stick up for Flynn, whatever he'd done. You know that,' Grace said gently. 'He didn't want me to show you this, but I had to say something. I couldn't know and not make sure you knew too.'

I said nothing. I just stared at her, still feeling numb.

'River, listen,' Emmi said briskly. 'The reason we've told you is to help you carry on getting over Flynn. I mean, you've seemed better this week, so I figured if you saw how he was moving on, then maybe *you'd* be able to move on as well.'

I barely heard her. 'Thanks, Grace,' I managed to say at last. 'I'm sorry this caused a row between you and James.'

'Are you all right, Riv?' Grace said, her tear-stained face screwed up with concern.

'Course,' I said. But in that moment, the full horror of it swamped me. Flynn had stolen Alex's iPad and others. He'd probably taken lots of other stuff too. He had loads of money and no intention of coming to see me. No, he was more interested in some girl in a bikini than me. Everything we'd said and done was tainted.

Everything was lies and pain.

My legs crumpled beneath me and I sank down onto the end of Emmi's bed. She was beside me in a second, her arms wrapped round me.

'I'm sorry, Riv. I know it's hard to hear like this, but it's better to face reality than live in a dream.' She paused. 'I haven't told Alex yet, but he's bound to see this and then Flynn will be in big trouble all over again. You're better off out of it.'

A hot, fat tear trickled down my face. My plan to

travel to Ireland to surprise him went through my head. How stupid was I?

Grace came over and knelt on the floor in front of me. She took my hand. 'We did the right thing telling you, didn't we? I mean you wanted to know, didn't you?'

I nodded. 'I ought to get home,' I said. 'Mum will have a fit if I don't get back soon.'

'No way.' Emmi gave my shoulder a shake. 'We're going out. All three of us.'

I looked up at her. 'Out where?' I said, dully. 'It's Monday night and I'm in enough trouble at home as it is.'

'Then a little more won't hurt, will it?' Emmi gave me a mischievous grin. 'Let's go to a club, just the three of us. Get all dressed up, yeah?'

'Tonight?' Grace looked scandalised. 'I can't, Emmi. I promised my parents I'd be home by nine.'

Emmi rolled her eyes. 'You *have* to come, Grace.'

I wiped my eyes. 'No she doesn't.'

Grace threw me a grateful glance. She looked so miserable – and it was all because she'd gone against her boyfriend to tell me something she knew I'd want to know about. That was real friendship. Just as Emmi's offer to take us out was her way of showing she cared.

'I don't mind coming,' Grace stammered. 'It's just there's something I need to do . . .'

'You want to speak to James?' I said.

Grace nodded.

I took out my phone. 'Let me talk to him first,' I said. It seemed like the least I could do.

'River?' James answered on the first ring, his voice all cautious. 'What's up?'

'Hi, James, I'm with Grace.'

Grace looked at me, her lip trembling.

'She's just been a really good friend to me – and she's really upset because you guys had a row so I'm putting her on now so you can make up.'

Without waiting for his response I handed the mobile to Grace. Her eyes widened but she took the phone and left Emmi's bedroom.

I looked around. Emmi was already fishing clothes out of her wardrobe.

'Whether Grace comes or not, we're definitely going, Riv,' she said. She took a low-cut black top off a hanger and shoved it towards me.

'You'll look great in this.'

I held up the top. It was pretty, but very revealing, and I could see already that it would make my boobs look huge.

'I don't know,' I began.

'Yes,' Emmi insisted. 'You *do* know. You're going

to wear the top. We're going to get out of here. We're going to have fun. Okay?'

I stared at her. Maybe she was right. Maybe this was just what I needed.

22

In the end, Grace did come with us – and so did James.

Emmi wasn't best pleased. She'd wanted this to be a girls' night out – but Grace looked so happy that everything was all right between her and James that it was impossible to be cross with her.

We got dressed up then sneaked out of Emmi's house. I switched off my phone. It was reckless of me to antagonise Mum like this, but right then I didn't care. Emmi bought some booze at the local shop that never asks for ID and we walked to the bus stop where James was already waiting.

He and Grace huddled together in the corner of the bus shelter, talking in smiles and low voices.

'James looks like one of those dogs with its tongue hanging out,' Emmi whispered.

I grinned. James, with his squishy, comfortable face and easy smile, *was* a bit like a dog. A golden retriever, maybe, or some kind of oversized spaniel. Anyway, he was clearly delighted to be making up with Grace.

I was happy for both of them. I tried not to think about Flynn. For a moment, as we got on the bus, I missed him so badly I could hardly breathe. Then I pushed it away. Tonight was about forgetting.

Tonight was about not thinking – just being.

We got into the club without any problem, mostly thanks to Emmi's highly flirtatious manner with the guy on the door. I'd been drinking all the way there – trying to get Flynn off my mind – so I felt quite light-headed by the time we arrived. It was still early in nightclub terms, not even ten-thirty, though I was aware Mum would have started freaking out an hour ago when I hadn't come home. At least when she tried to get hold of me at Emmi's she would discover both of us had run off, so hopefully she wouldn't think anything really bad had happened.

I pushed these thoughts out of my head with a final swig from Emmi's vodka bottle. I didn't want to think about Mum any more than I wanted to think about Flynn.

James bought a round of drinks then he and Grace

snuck away into a corner booth. Emmi and I hung around the bar, chatting. After a few minutes one of the guys there bought us each a second drink. We knocked them back then the three of us headed for the dance floor. Normally I feel self-conscious when I dance, but not that night.

I let myself go, moving with the music, not thinking, just being.

A few minutes later Emmi went to the Ladies and I went back the bar. The guy who'd bought our drinks followed me. As he ordered another round, I watched the flashing lights strobing across the dancers. The club was just starting to fill up. James and Grace were out of sight, snuggled in their corner. Emmi was still in the Ladies. The music was loud and insistent, the strong bass line vibrating through my feet and up my legs.

A long glass of coloured liquid appeared beside me. I took a sip. It was stronger than the last drink – some kind of cocktail – not really my thing. The guy who'd bought it placed another cocktail, for Emmi, on the counter, then swigged at his own beer.

'You never told me your name.' He smiled – a leering, sleazy kind of smile. 'I'm Ben.'

I looked him up and down.

On the plus side he was quite good-looking. A bit

pudgy maybe, but tall and well-built, with a strong chin and a great haircut. On the downside, he had cold eyes which had already snatched two long looks at my chest.

'Your name?' Ben asked again.

'Natalia,' I said.

Ben moved a little closer to me. 'I guess people call you Nat for short?'

I stifled a giggle. *Was that his idea of a chat-up line?* Flynn would eat this guy for breakfast.

A painful sob rose up inside me. I forced myself not to cry. I wasn't going to think about Flynn.

'Actually,' I said huskily, 'my friends call me Talia.'

'I see.' Ben nodded sagely, as if I'd just told him how to end world poverty. 'Another drink?'

I glanced down at the glass in my hand. It was nearly empty. I must have been drinking faster than I realised.

Keeping my eyes on Ben's face, I took a long swig, finishing the glass. 'Yes, please,' I said. 'I want to get off my face.'

Ben's cold eyes practically glinted. He handed me Emmi's cocktail. 'Looks like your friend has got her own drink.' I followed his gaze to where Emmi, fresh glass in hand, was chatting with a tall, good-looking guy I'd never seen before on the edge of the dance floor.

'D'you want to sit down for a moment?' Ben said.

'Sure.' Was I slurring? How embarrassing. Maybe it would be good to sit down for a bit. Ben led me over to an empty booth then squeezed in beside me.

The music was still loud, but it was easier to hear each other.

'You seen that new horror movie?' Ben said, looking sideways at my chest again. 'I can't remember the name, but it's the one with the headless zombies – *ZombieTown* or *ZombieWorld* . . . something like that . . .'

I shook my head, wondering vaguely why looking at my boobs was making him think about zombies. Ben proceeded to describe a battle scene from the movie in some detail. I tuned out totally after about ten seconds, concentrating only on my drink.

'Sounds great,' I said when he stopped to draw breath. I looked across the room. Grace and James were still deep in conversation. Emmi was still talking to the good-looking guy. He was leaning over her and she was smiling up at him.

Well, if Emmi could flirt with other people when she was going out with Alex, why shouldn't I flirt with Ben? After all, Flynn had lied to me. He didn't care about me.

Stop thinking about him.

214

I focused on Ben's face again. 'Thanks for the drinks,' I said.

'No problem.' A lustful smile curled across Ben's lips.

I wanted to tell him my boyfriend was really clever. Smart and witty and the most amazingly talented actor I'd ever met.

Except how could Flynn be my boyfriend anymore? Whatever he said, what could justify him gloating about stealing iPads? What could excuse that wad of money and the girl in the bikini? I fingered the silver bracelet around my wrist, feeling for the tiny heart that dangled from the chain. How ironic that it was still whole . . . while my real heart inside me was broken. No. How ironic that my real heart inside me was still beating, while—

'You feeling all right, Talia?' Ben said.

Who? Then I remembered my fake name and giggled. The room was spinning slightly. Ben's face loomed closer. There was a dark drink stain in the corner of his mouth. I stared at it, transfixed.

And then his mouth lunged at my face.

Contact. His lips were all full and fleshy. He started gnawing away at my face. It was so bad, it was almost funny. I pushed him away.

Ben drew back, looking confused. 'What's up, Talia?'

I giggled again. 'Just too much to drink,' I said.

I really wanted to go now. I started edging round the side of the booth Ben had pushed me into. But he followed me round.

'Don't go,' he said.

Before I could stop him his mouth was clamped over my lips again. I opened my mouth to say 'no', trying to push him away with my hands, but Ben simply kissed me harder. His tongue pushed inside my mouth.

Ugh. It was all thick and slimy, like a slug.

I gagged, which unfortunately Ben seemed to interpret as me getting into the kiss. He ran his hands up my top, groping roughly at me.

Now I thought I really *was* going to be sick. It was disgusting. *He* was disgusting. This time I managed to push him away and wriggle out of the booth. Ben grabbed at my hand, but I shook him off and headed for James and Grace.

The floor seemed to sway underneath me. I was staggering as I walked.

I was suddenly reminded of the evening when I'd got drunk and Flynn had seen me be sick. I'd wanted him to kiss me and he hadn't, but he'd rubbed my arms to warm them in the cold night air.

Tears started streaming down my face. I heard Ben's voice behind me. 'What's going on?'

'Go away,' I said. 'Please.'

'Right.' His voice hardened. 'Just after the drinks, were you?'

I turned around. 'No,' I said. 'I don't know.' I really was slurring now. 'I'm sorry but I'm not interested.'

'Yeah? Why's that? Cos you've had enough now?'

No. It's cos you're stupid and you've got a tongue like a slug. And . . . and you're not him.

Ben swore loudly then stomped away. I slid to the floor, my body racked with sobs. Why had Flynn lied to me? I didn't care what he'd done, but I couldn't bear the thought that he didn't love me.

'River?'

I looked up.

James was leaning over me, looking concerned. 'Are you okay?' He frowned. 'Did that guy upset you?'

I got up, wiping my tears furiously.

'I'm fine.' I took an extremely unsteady step past him then nearly fell again. James grabbed my arm. Someone else caught me round the waist.

I looked around. It was Emmi. Grace was here too, her eyes anxious. They led me over to a seat and let me lie there, my head spinning for a few moments while they spoke to each other. I couldn't hear what they were saying, but soon James was back, tugging me upright again.

217

He put his arm round me and helped me walk out of the club. Grace trotted along on my other side. She was speaking rapidly in my ear, but I could only take in about half of what she said.

'You're in such a state . . . Emmi's met up with some guy she knows, so she's going to stay for a bit but we're going to get a cab . . . take you home . . . I'm calling your mum . . .'

'Home?' I just managed to get the word out.

'Of course,' James muttered. 'I can't leave you like this.'

I looked at him, sure I knew what he was thinking: *Flynn wouldn't like me to leave you like this.*

'Don't s'pose he cares,' I mumbled, pulling my arm away.

James frowned. 'I don't think that's true, River.'

'Whatever.' I bit my lip.

James steered me onto the pavement. It was a chilly night, but although I could see the skin on my arms raised in goosebumps, I didn't actually feel cold. It took a few minutes to find a cab. James helped me and Grace into the back and the three of us sat down in a row, with James in the middle. I closed my eyes. My head was spinning but I didn't feel sick.

James and Grace chatted quietly for a few minutes then the cab grew silent. I opened my eyes and looked around.

Grace was fast asleep in the far corner of the back seat.

'Are you all right, River?' James asked.

I stared at his kind, anxious face. Tears pricked at my eyes.

'Fine,' I lied.

'I don't believe he did it,' James said quietly. 'Flynn, I mean.'

I sniffed. 'Don't want to talk about him.'

I looked round at Grace again. She was still sound asleep, her lips slightly parted and her breathing steady and regular.

'You and Grace are so great together,' I said, squeezing James's arm. 'You do love her, don't you? Because she's nuts about you and I think you're both lovely.' I beamed up at him.

Poor James looked extremely embarrassed. He gazed past me, out of the window. We were speeding down half-empty streets. I had no idea where we were. Everything felt surreal. The window beside me was a little way open, wind rushing through across the top of my hair.

'I miss him,' I said.

Damn. Why had I said that? *Stop it, River.*

But I couldn't stop.

'D'you think Flynn's going out with that girl in the picture?' I clutched at James's arm more tightly.

'No, I'm sure he isn't,' James said.

'James.' He recoiled as I drew closer. 'Are you really sure?'

'Well . . . no,' James stammered. 'But he's . . . he's all into you.'

Yeah right. What else was James going to say.

My eyes welled up with tears. 'Oh, God,' I wailed.

'River?' James voice was pleading. 'Please just calm down. I'm sure Flynn still—'

'Don't,' I spat. 'Don't say he still loves me. Don't say he still anything.' Fury coiled itself in my throat. 'He's a liar and a thief and . . .'

'He never—'

'Don't defend him.' I broke down again, squeezing my eyes tight shut. The cab started spinning. I could feel myself sliding down the seat. I looked up. I was slumped half across James. I reached up, hooked my arm round his neck and hauled myself up.

'Oh James,' I wept, leaning against his chest. 'I love him so much I think he's made me allergic to other men. Seriously. That boy earlier, *he* tried to kiss me and it was disgusting.'

James laughed nervously and patted me on the back.

I shuddered, remembering Ben's slug tongue.

That kiss had made me want to vomit. Suppose all kisses did that from now on?

And then I had an idea. A very bad idea. I looked up. 'Let me kiss *you*, James,' I said. 'Just to see. Not a big one, just a little kiss to make sure it doesn't make me feel sick, like it did with ... with ... Slug Tongue.'

James stared at me in horror. 'River, you cannot be ...'

'Go on,' I wheedled drunkenly. I moved in on him, my mouth just centimetres away from his. 'Just so I can see it doesn't make me wanna puke.'

'You want to kiss me to see if it makes you feel sick?'

'No. *Not* sick. Oh for goodness sake.' I pressed my lips against his. Neither of us moved. I started laughing. And as my mouth relaxed, it sort of moved against James's – like a reflex action. Then his moved against mine. And we were kissing. His lips were smooth and soft. And the kiss was ... well ... nice. Not hot. Nowhere near as passionate as Flynn's kisses, but still nice.

I had a sudden memory of Grace telling me and Emmi that James was a good kisser.

Grace.

I sprang away from James and slapped my hands over my mouth.

'Oh God,' I hissed, frantically. 'I am so sorry, James.'

We both looked round at Grace. She was still fast asleep, curled up in the far corner of the cab.

I shrank into my own corner, completely horror-struck. How could I have done that? How could I have been so selfish that I forgot James was going out with my friend . . . my good friend. I was a terrible, evil, loathsome person. I was scum.

I felt James's hand on my shoulder and shrank away.

'River.' He sounded half angry, half amused. 'Shut up.'

I stared at him. Had I been saying those thoughts out loud?

'You're not terrible or evil or whatever,' he grinned. 'You're just ridiculously drunk.'

'I'm sorry,' I whimpered.

'Don't be.' James shrugged, his cheeks scarlet. 'Look, forget it. Seriously. I mean it. Forget it. It's not a big deal. Okay?'

I knew what he was saying. *Don't say anything to Grace.*

I was too drunk still to work out whether that was the right thing to do or not, but I nodded anyway.

James sat back. Then he glanced over again. 'Just

tell me one thing,' he said. 'And we'll never mention this again.'

I nodded.

He lowered his voice. 'Did you feel sick just now? It's just I'd like to think I was doing better than Slug Tongue.'

23

I woke up the next morning racked with guilt. My first instinct was to rush around to Grace's house and confess what I'd done. But as I thought it through I realised how selfish that would be. However hard I tried to explain to Grace that the kiss had been an accident that had only lasted a nano-second, I knew all she would hear was that it had happened in the first place. A confession would probably ruin everything between her and James, not to mention our own friendship. Plus, James had asked me not to tell her because it was meaningless. Which it was. 'A few seconds of lip contact' – as Flynn had once described such kisses – that had led nowhere.

Anyway, the last thing I needed was a bust-up with my friends. Mum had been white-faced when James and Grace had delivered me home. I'd been expecting her to shout at me, but she just helped me upstairs and put me to bed saying we'd 'talk in the morning'.

My head was sore but I didn't feel too bad, considering. I sat up and glanced at my clock. It was nearly eleven a.m. Mum had obviously let me sleep in rather than go to school. I heard her footsteps on the stairs and braced myself.

I'd gone out without leaving any message. I'd got drunk. I'd come home in the middle of the night.

She was going to be furious. And I couldn't blame her.

I looked down at my hands in my lap as she walked in. She crossed the room silently and sat on the edge of the bed.

'River?'

I looked up.

Mum was dressed for work but not wearing any make-up. There were dark shadows under her eyes. A tray with soup and toast was in her lap.

'I brought you something to eat,' she said, handing me the tray.

I took it and balanced it on the bed. 'Thank you.' I held my breath, waiting for the torrent of rage to rain down on me.

There was a long pause.

'You can't do this anymore,' Mum said

eventually, her voice flat, but calm. 'D'you have any idea how worried I was when I spoke to Emmi's mum and found out you girls had run off somewhere?'

She didn't sound angry at all. More exhausted.

I looked away.

'I'm sorry,' I mumbled. 'I didn't mean to upset you.'

'So you say.' Mum sighed. 'But there have to be consequences.'

I nodded. What was coming now?

'Your dad has asked for you to go and stay at the commune once we get to the Easter holidays. I'd send you now, but I'm aware you've got practice tests for your GCSEs this week, haven't you?'

Jeez. In all the turmoil over Flynn I'd completely forgotten the tests that started tomorrow. Oh, well, I'd get them over then it wouldn't be too long to the end of term. Maybe it wouldn't even be so bad to spend a couple of weeks with Dad.

Mum sighed again. 'I thought it best to let you sleep it off this morning. You can do some work in your room, go to school tomorrow.'

'Okay,' I said.

'Grace and James told me about Flynn's Facebook page.' Mum hesitated. 'I hope it shows you that you've had a lucky escape from that boy.'

I looked down. The sick, miserable feeling I'd had yesterday surged through me again, filling every cell in my body. I wanted to stick up for Flynn but the words lodged in my throat. After all, it was possible Mum was right. Not that I wanted to admit it to her.

Mum reached across the duvet and took one of my hands in hers. 'I know you don't believe this, but I understand how you feel.' She squeezed my hand. 'I know how hard it is to be disappointed and let down . . . to be in love and it to not work out . . .'

My cheeks burned.

'So I'm not going to give you a hard time about last night. But I do expect your solemn promise that you will never run off like that without telling me. Not ever again. Deal?'

I nodded. 'Deal,' I mumbled. Jeez, why was she being so nice? The miserable sick feeling was like a dead weight inside me.

'Good.' Mum laid my hand down and patted it. 'Eat your soup. I'm off to work in a few minutes. You get on with your revision.'

She stood up. And I remembered.

'Mum, I left all my school stuff at Emmi's,' I said. 'I need to go round there and pick it up.' This was perfectly true, but I was worried, under the circumstances, that Mum would think I was trying to trick her.

'No problem,' Mum said. 'I'll drive you over once you've eaten. Emmi's mother is in . . . I spoke to her earlier. You can go in, pick up your stuff and I'll bring you back home.'

'Thanks,' I said, wondering again why she was being so nice.

Mum disappeared into her room and I nibbled at my toast and sipped at my soup. Though I hadn't felt hungry when I'd started eating, the food made me feel better. After a few minutes Mum returned, now wearing make-up.

She took my tray.

'Get dressed,' she said. 'I've spoken to Emmi's mum. We're going over there in five minutes.'

I got out of bed and slowly dragged on a pair of sweats and my trainers. My phone was lying on the floor where I'd left it last night. I switched it on.

It vibrated immediately. Flynn was calling.

I stared, shocked, at his name on the screen. This was too sudden. I needed to speak to him, but I wasn't prepared. What was I going to say? And Mum would be back in a second, expecting me to be ready to go out.

Flynn was the last person she'd want to find me talking to.

My hand hovered over the buttons,

'River!' Mum yelled up the stairs. 'Let's go!'

The phone vibrated again. No way could I speak to him right now. I pressed the red button to cut off the call, then turned off the phone.

'Coming!' I yelled. I grabbed a jumper and scurried out of the room.

Mum talked about work as we drove to Emmi's. I didn't say much. My head still hurt – moving about wasn't helping – and it was easiest just to let her chatter on.

'So it's not just the Easter holidays. Your dad wants you to spend the whole summer at the commune,' Mum said, changing tack. 'I think it's a good idea for you to have a total break from your life here.' She threw an anxious sideways glance at me. 'You're not going to be difficult about that, are you, River?'

'No, Mum. It's fine,' I said, numbly.

I tried to focus on what she had asked. In some ways the idea of endless weeks on the commune filled me with horror. But the idea of being holed up with Mum all summer was worse. Anyway, what did it really matter what I did?

Flynn wasn't who I thought he was. I couldn't trust him. He had changed and I had to cope with that. The irony was, of course, that the only person I wanted to help me cope was Flynn. I wanted his arms around me more than anything.

Mum drew up outside Emmi's house. 'I have to make a work call,' she said. 'I'll wait here. Don't be too long.'

'Okay.' I hauled myself out of the car and trudged up the steps to Emmi's front door. Emmi's mum let me in. She looked harassed.

'I had a quick look in Emmi's room but it was such a mess, as usual . . .' She sighed. 'I couldn't work out which were your things and which were hers, so you'd better have a look yourself.'

'Did Emmi get home okay then?' I said, feeling awkward as I walked to the stairs. Was Emmi in trouble for sneaking out too?

'Yes, she got back about one,' Emmi's mum said. 'I had no idea she'd even gone out, but after your mum called, Louise said Emmi had told her, so at least . . .' She sighed. 'A friend of Emmi's brought her home in a taxi,' she went on. 'I suppose she was safe, but she shouldn't have gone on a school night, though she was up again all bright and breezy this morning, so . . . Anyway, you girls *must* tell us where you are. You have no idea how we worry.' She sighed again.

I shook my head as I made my way up the stairs to Emmi's room. Thanks to Emmi's parents being fairly slack and her older sister Louise being prepared to cover for her, Emmi never seemed to get into as much trouble as I did. Plus she always managed to charm her way out of things. Look at the way she'd got the guy she'd bumped into at the club to bring her home in a cab.

I stood in the doorway of Emmi's room.

'I'll leave you to it,' her mum said. She drifted away towards the bathroom and I gazed around the bedroom. It was, certainly, in a terrible mess. Clothes were strewn everywhere, mostly on the carpet around the bed. I wandered over and started looking for my school uniform and bag full of textbooks.

I couldn't see them anywhere. I was certain I'd just dumped them on the floor, but perhaps Emmi had shoved them somewhere out of the way.

I had a quick look under the bed, then yanked open Emmi's walk-in closet. It was, if anything, even messier than the rest of the bedroom. I saw my school bag straight away, but there was still no sign of my uniform. I sat on the floor, my head throbbing again from my exertions, examining a huge pile of jumpers. Nothing. I lay down, flat on the floor, peering into the corners of the closet. There, right at the back, under the racks full of shoes, was a heap of school skirts and shirts. Had my stuff got mixed in with Emmi's?

I crawled closer, pulling the bits and pieces of uniform towards me. I examined the various skirts and shirts – none of them were mine. Only one last shirt remained. It was half hidden behind a small wooden box that I vaguely remembered once seeing at the end of Emmi's bed when we were younger. As I reached around behind the box to free the shirt, I caught a flash of silver on some dark blue cloth. The silver was a crest, a school crest. But not ours. It was the logo for St Cletus's, the school that Flynn and Alex and James went to. Curious, I tugged at the cloth – it was an old-style PE bag. Our school didn't use such things but I knew the boys were supposed to keep their football boots in them.

I pulled the bag properly into view. There was something inside it.

Forgetting my search for my uniform and Mum waiting outside in the car, I opened the bag then gasped, unable to believe what was inside.

24

It was an iPad. I turned it over. The metal on the back was engraved with Alex's name.

What was Alex's missing iPad doing here, shoved out of sight at the back of Emmi's walk-in closet? Had *Emmi* taken it? Had she hidden it here?

My mind reeled with the implications. If Alex's iPad was here, then it surely proved Flynn hadn't stolen it. But why would *Emmi* steal it? Alex was her boyfriend. The answer hit me like a fist. Emmi must have taken the iPad in order to put the blame on Flynn. *No. Surely* Emmi wouldn't do that? She'd never liked him but it was unthinkable that she would go this far.

Wasn't it?

'River, how are you doing?' Emmi's mum's voice echoed towards me from across the landing.

'Fine.' I scrambled to my feet, wrapping the PE bag around the iPad. I shoved it into my school bag

233

and stood up. I walked out of the closet as Emmi's mum appeared in the bedroom doorway.

'Find everything?' she asked.

As she spoke, I caught sight of my school shoes, tie, shirt and skirt in a neat pile just to the right of the door. I hadn't noticed before, but Emmi had obviously left them there for me this morning.

'Yes, thanks.' I held out my school bag to show Emmi's mum then picked up the pile of clothes and followed her out of the room.

Emmi's mum chattered away as we went downstairs, but I didn't hear a word. I said goodbye, still in a daze, and got back in the car with Mum. She was on the phone, but ended the call as I sat down in the passenger seat, my bag on my lap.

'I'm just going to drop you at home, River,' she said. 'Then I have to shoot off to work. I'll be back at six. We'll have dinner. Then, perhaps, we can talk . . .'

'Sure,' I said, blankly.

I *had* to speak to Flynn. It was all I could think about: he was innocent of stealing Alex's iPad. My mind kept going over how he'd rung me earlier and how I'd just let my mobile ring then switched it off because I couldn't face him. I needed to call him back straight away.

As soon as Mum dropped me at home I rushed up to my room and switched on my phone. Flynn had left a voice message. I listened to it, my heart in my mouth.

'River, why aren't you answering?' He sounded desperate. 'Listen, they've set me up . . . they've hacked my Facebook page, I know you'll have seen it. You *have* to believe me. I didn't put that picture there. It's not even real, it's Photoshopped. It's a fake. It's a lie, just like the stuff about the iPads. Please, River, please believe me, please call back.'

A sob rose in my chest. Flynn had never gone anywhere near Alex's iPad. I had the proof now – and yet, if I hadn't found it, I wasn't sure whether I would have believed Flynn. Guilt for my mistrust filled me to my fingertips.

I sat on my bed, emotions tumbling through me. I felt angry with Emmi and shame over not totally believing Flynn and still completely confused about what had actually happened. I took a deep breath. The most important thing was that I talked to Flynn and told him I believed him.

I called his number. But the phone didn't connect. Not even to his voicemail. What did that mean?

I tried again. And again. And again. Not caring whether Mum did a spot check later and got suspicious about the number I was dialling.

But there was no reply.

I went online. Flynn's Facebook page had

disappeared too. Well, it would have if it had been hacked and he'd reported it.

But it left me with no way to contact him.

Panic swirled in my stomach.

I had to reach him. But how?

Maybe James would have another number. After what happened in the taxi last night, he was the last person I wanted to speak to right now but it might be worth a try. Except that it was almost midday so James would be at school, just like Emmi and Grace.

School. My chest tightened as I thought about how everyone at Flynn's school believed the worst of him. Well, they weren't going to any longer. I grabbed my keys and a coat and, with Alex's iPad tucked under my arm, I headed to St Cletus's.

It took over thirty minutes to get there. I tried several times on the way to reach Flynn again but the number was still completely unobtainable. I was half expecting the school to be awash with boys on their lunch break but, thankfully, the entrance hall was quiet as the receptionist let me in.

'Can I help you?' she asked politely.

'I have information about a . . . a theft from one of the students here,' I stammered. 'I'd like to see the Head, please.'

The receptionist stared at me. 'What's this about?' she asked.

'I want to talk to the headteacher,' I repeated stubbornly.

My head still hurt and the dark, sick, miserable feeling in my gut was now a knot of intense anxiety, but surely Flynn's phone would ring soon – and when I spoke to him I wanted to be able to tell him that the very first thing I'd done on finding the iPad was to clear his name.

I waited another ten minutes, rehearsing exactly what I was going to say. I'd met Mr McClure, the St Cletus's head, on a couple of occasions, most recently when he'd introduced the performances of *Romeo and Juliet* that I'd acted in with Flynn last term. He was short with sandy hair, round glasses and a warm smile. The boys said he had a really mean streak, but I'd never seen any evidence of that myself. He'd always seemed nice – and approachable.

'River Armstrong?' Mr McClure was standing in front of me. He smiled. 'I thought I remembered the name. You were in our play last term, weren't you?'

I nodded, clutching the bag with the iPad.

'Now, what's this about? Shouldn't you be at school?'

I stood up slowly, then drew the iPad out of the PE bag.

'I found this. It belongs to a boy who comes here. Alex Barker. He thought . . . people thought that Flynn, Patrick Flynn, took it.' I handed the iPad to Mr McClure.

I wanted to say Flynn was my boyfriend, but that was far too embarrassing. Mr McClure turned the iPad over. As he read the engraving on the back his eyebrows shot up.

'This was reported missing several weeks ago,' Mr McClure mused. 'Where did you find it?'

'At a friend's house,' I said. 'A friend of mine and Alex's.' My throat felt tight. I'd come here only thinking about proving Flynn's innocence, but now I was standing in front of Mr McClure I realised that if I said any more, I'd get Emmi into massive trouble.

No matter what she'd done, I couldn't do that.

Mr McClure's eyebrows rose further. He strode over to the receptionist and asked her to have Alex removed from his class and brought straight to his office. Then he asked me to go into the office and wait with him.

The room was small and rather stuffy. A large bookshelf groaned with files and the desk in the centre was also heavily cluttered with papers. Mr

McClure pointed to one of the chairs. 'Sit there, please.' He had totally lost his warm smile.

I sat down, my hands shaking. Now what was going to happen?

25

A minute later, Alex knocked on the door and was ordered inside. He did a double take when he saw me, then another when Mr McClure produced his iPad.

'River says she found this at a mutual friend's house.' Mr McClure fixed Alex with a stern stare. 'Should we call your parents and the police to report its discovery?'

I could feel my cheeks burning. I hadn't anticipated this. Alex's face went bright red too.

'Oh,' he said. 'I see.'

I stared at him. There was something wrong. He didn't look in the slightest bit shocked or surprised.

Mr McClure turned to me. 'Exactly where did you find it, River?' he asked.

'Er . . .' I couldn't dump Emmi in it. 'Er . . .'

'You said a mutual friend?' Mr McClure prompted with a frown.

I looked at the floor.

'Oh my goodness, was it Emmi's house?' Alex said.

I glanced up, my mouth falling open. How did he know?

'Er, yes.'

'Right.' Alex turned back to Mr McClure, his face still bright red. 'Emmi's my girlfriend, sir. She's a friend of River's. I must have left the iPad there by . . . by mistake. Er, thanks for finding it, River.'

Was Alex seriously expecting us to believe this was all an *accident*? There was no outrage in his voice – nor any confusion. Just massive embarrassent. And it hit me . . . There was only one way he could have known the iPad was in Emmi's bedroom:

He'd *hidden* it there.

Mr McClure looked sceptically at the pair of us then asked me to wait outside while he talked privately with Alex.

I did as I was told. Five minutes later, Mr McClure reappeared. He thanked me for coming to the school to return the lost property. 'You did the right thing, River,' he said with a smile as he walked me to the door.

'This means Flynn didn't take the iPad,' I blurted out. 'You do see that, don't you?'

241

'Yes, I see.' Mr McClure smiled again, but I got the distinct impression it didn't make any difference to his overall feelings about Flynn.

I had no choice but to leave. I wandered to St Cletus's school gates. I remembered the first time I'd ever been here, for the audition for *Romeo and Juliet* . . . The day I'd met Flynn. As I reached the gates, I took out my phone and tried him again. Still no response. I scrolled to Emmi's number. Had she known about the iPad? I wasn't sure anymore. I hesitated, lost in thought. Her phone would almost certainly be on silent right now, while she was at school, which meant I'd have to leave a message. And I wanted to see her face when I asked her about it.

'River?' Alex's voice brought me back to the present moment. I turned as he ran across the tarmac towards me.

The wind blew a strand of hair in my eyes.

'I only have a second,' Alex said, his own blond fringe ruffling in the breeze. 'Mr McClure told me to go straight back to class but I had to speak to you first. Please don't tell Emmi about this.'

I frowned, brushing my hair out of my eyes. 'Don't tell Emmi about me finding your iPad in her bedroom closet?' I could hear the bitterness in my voice. 'Doesn't Emmi know already?'

'No.' Alex shook his head vehemently. 'Emmi doesn't know. *Honestly*. Look, if I explain what happened, will you promise not to say anything?'

I nodded slowly. 'Go on . . .'

Alex held up the iPad. 'I got this for Christmas but then the new version came out and I wanted an upgrade for my birthday but Mum and Dad said no, it was too soon, so I waited a few weeks then I pretended it had been stolen so my dad would buy a new one with the insurance.'

I stared at him, horrifed. I'd told some lies to Mum and Dad in my time, but nothing on that kind of scale. 'You *pretended* it had been *stolen*?' I said.

'Yes, I was worried my parents would find it if I hid it in my house, so I stashed it in Emmi's closet. I was going to get it out and sell it later but . . .'

'You accused Flynn of stealing it.' My mouth fell open. I couldn't believe what I was hearing. 'You let him take the blame.'

Alex looked away, his face covered with shame. 'I know, but Flynn's an . . .' He paused. 'I know he's your boyfriend but nobody likes him. He's rude and violent and . . .' He paused again. 'I shouldn't have blamed him, but it's not like I was the only one. Flynn was *always* getting in trouble.'

'Was it you who hacked his Facebook page?' I demanded.

'No, that wasn't me.' Alex met my gaze. 'I have no idea who did that but it was probably someone else Flynn annoyed. I get that you see him differently, but—'

'Don't say any more,' I interrupted. I didn't want to hear another word about how the rest of the world saw Flynn. I lived with the consequences of that every day.

Alex nodded. 'Okay.' He still looked desperate. 'Okay . . . so you won't say anything to Emmi . . . you promise? I'm going to be in enough trouble when my parents realise I just "lost" this, that it wasn't really stolen.'

I bit my lip. I felt angry enough to broadcast what Alex had done to everyone I knew, but what good would it do?

'Fine,' I said. 'I won't say where I found it, so long as you make sure you tell Emmi you *have* found it, so she and everyone else will know Flynn had nothing to do with it.'

'Deal.' Alex thanked me, looking relieved, then walked back into school.

I went home. I tried to study, but it was impossible. Emmi phoned later to see if I was okay. I kept my word to Alex and told her nothing about the iPad. She mentioned it herself, explaining it had turned up after all 'in Alex's locker at school'.

I pointed out this clearly let Flynn off the hook – as did the fact that his Facebook account had obviously been hacked – but it made no difference. Emmi was just as disposed to think badly of him today as she had been yesterday.

The same was true of Mum who, as promised, sat me down for a Big Talk when she got home from work. I submitted to a long lecture which covered personal responsibility, problem drinking and the importance of Moving On. The fact that Flynn was innocent of the theft didn't matter to Mum, any more than it had to Emmi or Mr McClure.

In their eyes he was difficult and unlikeable and I was better off without him.

And I *was* without him. I tried over and over again to call – but his number stayed unobtainable. By the time I went to school the next day I was beside myself with worry. What on earth had happened to him? Was he okay? I'd called James – who didn't have another number for him – and even left a message at the hairdressing salon where Siobhan used to work. I was hoping that the owner, Mr Goode, would give me Gary's mobile number, and that I might be able to get hold of Flynn through him.

I had to switch off my phone for the whole afternoon in order to take the history and English tests we'd been set. I knew I'd done badly – it was just so hard to focus, not knowing what had happened to Flynn.

After the exams I chatted to the girls for a while. Emmi was offhand about the tests, making out she'd done no work at all and didn't care about the results. Grace was typically anxious – worried that in spite of all her revision, she'd answered the questions poorly. Emmi suggested we walked to the Broadway and bought ice creams. It was a sunny day – the warmest of the year so far.

I said I had to get home and left them to it. The truth was, I was desperate to try Flynn again. But his number was still unavailable and, so far, Mr Goode hadn't returned my call either. I took a detour to the park. It really was a beautiful day – a brilliant sun burned down from a clear blue sky. I felt deeply, desperately sad.

Where was Flynn? Why hadn't he called me? He must know his phone wasn't working. Surely he could have borrowed a mobile to get hold of me if he'd really wanted to?

I strolled across the concrete play area at the start of the park and onto the grassy square. It was busier than I'd seen it for ages, thanks to the fabulous weather. I found an empty bench between two groups of mothers with toddlers and pushchairs. It was the place we'd had that row just before Caitlin's first Holy Communion and almost immediately opposite the café where Flynn and I had met on our very first date.

I hugged my knees to my chest and squeezed my eyes tight shut, trying to block out the memories.

I didn't hear his footsteps. I don't even know how long he was standing there. But I sensed someone looking at me and glanced up.

I gasped.

Flynn was leaning against a tree with his arms folded, smiling at me.

26

It was him. It was really him. He held me for a moment with those green-gold eyes of his. I stared, hardly believing he was real. He looked good. *So* good. His hair was slightly longer than when I'd last seen him and he had new clothes on – jeans and a T-shirt I didn't recognise.

These thoughts registered in a fraction of a second. And then we were both moving, rushing towards each other, the sun and the park and the grass at our feet forgotten. I hurled myself into his arms.

He held me tight.

'Oh, River.' His voice was soft and strong in my ear. 'I had to see you. I had to talk to you.' His voice broke and he pulled away, holding my face in his hands. His eyes bored into me, as intense as I'd ever seen.

I realised I was holding my breath. I laughed at

the thought that Flynn literally took my breath away.

'What?' Flynn's face clouded with misunderstanding. 'Don't laugh, Riv. I didn't steal anything. Not *ever*. And my account was hacked into and that photo was faked up and—'

'I know.' I put my finger on his lips to stop him talking. 'I know you didn't do any of those things.'

Flynn nodded. But his forehead was still creased with a deep frown.

'You didn't take my call yesterday . . .' he said.

'Only because my mum was . . . was there, waiting for me,' I said. 'I tried to call you as soon as I was on my own, but your phone was switched off or something.' I kept my gaze steady as I spoke, but inside I felt a stab of guilt. I wasn't telling the whole truth . . . at the time I'd mistrusted Flynn. It was only after I found Alex's iPad that I tried to call him back.

'As soon as you didn't pick up I knew I had to get here,' Flynn said. He pulled me into another hug, his lips brushing against my ear as he spoke. 'I was so sick of being there anyway. I hated it. *Hated*. Whoever it was – Alex or whoever – hacking my Facebook page was the last straw. I had a bit of money saved up and I went straight to this guy I'd met in Dub and sold him my handset.'

I gasped. 'You sold your *phone*?'

Flynn nodded. 'It all added up to just enough money. I left a note for Mum then headed to the airport. I waited for a standby flight. It took *forever* but I got on one at last. Soon as I got here this afternoon I went to your school,' Flynn said. 'Everyone was coming out of doing tests. I kept asking. Eventually someone said they thought you'd come in this direction . . .'

I pulled back and stared at him, open-mouthed.

'You came all this way just to make sure I knew you weren't a thief or a liar?' I said. 'All this way? For me?'

A beat passed. The sun shone fierce in the sky. Flynn moved closer, the same fire burning bright in his eyes.

'I'd do *anything* for you,' he said.

His face was just above mine. I knew the shape and lines of it better than my own.

'I love you,' he said.

His lips brushed mine. And the dead weight that I'd carried in my chest since he'd gone dissolved as we kissed.

At last we pulled apart and I opened my eyes. The breeze was soft and warm on my skin, the air perfumed with the fresh scent of mown grass. All around us, the happy shrieks of small children rose into the air.

I felt alive, like the world was in colour again.

'Oh Riv, you don't know how much it means, knowing you believed in me.' Flynn's face was wreathed in a shy smile.

The world darkened slightly, as if a shadow had appeared over our heads. I hugged him again, trying to ignore it. The truth was I *hadn't* believed in him. I had doubted everything – that he was honest, that he was true . . .

'Of course I believed in you,' I said. We held hands and strolled across the park to a bench. As we walked, I explained how I'd found Alex's iPad in Emmi's bedroom and taken it to St Cletus's. 'Alex said Emmi didn't know he'd hidden the iPad there and I promised him I wouldn't tell her but . . .'

Flynn swore. His face filled with fury. 'That means Alex completely set me up.'

'I know.' My heartbeat quickened. I didn't want Flynn to get in a bad mood now, not while he was being so sweet and loving. 'But I've made sure Alex tells everyone that it turned up, so they know *you* didn't take it.'

'It won't make any difference,' Flynn said with an angry grunt, sitting down on the bench.

I sat down beside him, feeling troubled. He was right. Mum and Emmi's reactions were proof of that.

251

'How long will you be here?' I asked, hoping to change the subject.

Flynn said nothing. His face grew even more thunderous.

'Flynn?' I said, feeling uneasy. 'When will you have to go back to Ireland?'

'I'm not. I couldn't have stood it there another day anyway.'

What? 'You're not going back?' My mouth fell open.

'No,' Flynn said, folding his arms in that stubborn way of his I knew so well. 'I'll stay here. Get a job, like we talked about before.'

'But . . .' A thousand difficulties and complications filled my head. 'But where will you live? How will you do your A levels?'

'I'll stay with friends to start with until I can afford a place of my own. And I'll find a sixth form college where I can do my A2s – the coursework, the exams. I'll go to work around the lessons and if I have to miss classes I'll catch up.'

I stared at him. It sounded impossible, but I knew Flynn well enough by now to realise that if anyone could make such a plan work, it was him.

'Okay,' I said slowly. 'But even if you sort out school, what will we tell Mum and Dad to make them let me see you properly again?'

Flynn shrugged. 'I don't know,' he said.

I took a deep breath. 'Wherever you go and whatever you do, the same bad things will happen so long as you keep getting angry all the time,' I said.

Flynn shot a sharp look at me. 'I don't get angry all the time,' he said, his voice rising.

'Yes, you do. You're getting angry now.'

'I'm *not*.'

'You *are*, and all I'm asking is how we're going to convince my parents you've really changed when—?'

'I don't freakin' know how!' Flynn snapped. He leaped up from the bench and paced across to the nearest tree.

My chest tightened. Here it was again, that terrible temper still raging in his heart. I glanced around us. A nearby group of mums and toddlers were watching him anxiously.

Flynn strode back to where I was still sitting on the bench. He glared down at me. 'I don't have all the freakin' answers, River, but we'll work it out as we go along. I thought you believed in me?'

I opened my mouth to point out that by getting so furious he was totally proving my argument, when Flynn sank onto the bench and bowed his head.

'I'm sorry,' he mumbled, his fury vanishing as quickly as it had flared up. 'I know you believe in me, I just . . . I have no idea how anything is going to work out. The stupid thing I did a few days ago, the thing I mentioned on the phone – it was a fight . . . at my new school. The guys there are just as big idiots as the ones at St Cletus's.'

'Right,' I said. My heart sank. I'd been so afraid that Flynn had changed, that he'd stopped loving me. But the reality was, in its way, just as bad. Flynn hadn't changed at all. He was still getting into fights and blaming everyone else for making him angry.

Flynn took my hand from the bench where it rested and held it in his. 'I will make it work,' he said. 'I will find a way. I realised when I was in Ireland that my first priority, before everything else, is to be with you, for us to be together. That's the most important thing.' He hesitated. 'It's the same for you, isn't it?'

I gulped, my stomach cartwheeling. 'Yes, except . . .' I paused. It was always like this around Flynn, I realised. Huge emotions consuming me, leaving no room for anything else. I was tired of the tidal wave of feeling that swamped me then pulled away again, leaving me exhausted.

Flynn pulled me gently to my feet. He pressed his hands around my waist and drew me towards him. 'Except what?' he said.

His eyes were so full of passion and I wanted him so badly. This was what I had dreamed of for months. And yet . . . of all the challenges facing Flynn right now, the biggest by far was one he couldn't see . . . and one I didn't want to have to live with anymore.

'River?' Flynn's eyes searched my face. 'I want to be with you, River. That's why I came back. I tried to make it work in Ireland, but I can't. I spent all my money getting here. And I'm not going back. I don't care about anything else. Just you, River.'

He bent closer, his eyes pulling me towards him. My head was spinning. I could feel my insides melting as he gazed at me. And yet . . . and yet . . .

'No.' I pulled away, stepping back across the grass. I looked round the park at the straggle of mums and toddlers now heading towards the exit.

Flynn made everything sound so reasonable. As if the anger and the mistrust and all the distance between us over the past few months could be wiped away with a kiss and an apology. 'No,' I repeated, this time more forcefully. 'You can't just say you're sorry and expect that to make everything all right in the future.'

'I *can* make everything all right. Listen, Riv—'

'No. *You* listen.' I took a deep breath. 'Sometimes your being cross about things is justified, but a lot of the time you get angry over nothing.'

Flynn stared at me. He didn't speak.

'Look at how you reacted just because I went to that party with Emmi and Alex,' I went on. 'You hung up on me. And before *that* it was difficult because I was scared of upsetting you and us arguing when we couldn't see each other to make up. And before *that* . . . well there was always your temper. It was the reason for you getting into fights and it made . . . it makes . . . me feel you're always on the verge of freaking out.'

'But . . .' Flynn's expression was guarded. 'What are you saying, Riv?'

'I'm saying that Mum and Dad were right about you being out of control,' I went on, meeting his gaze head on. 'And I can't handle it. I don't *want* to handle it. I mean, what if we're together and everything's great and then something happens to annoy you and you flare up again for no reason.'

'There's always a reason.' Flynn's eyes burned into me. 'I thought you understood.'

'It's not enough for me to understand,' I insisted. 'And I don't always. Sometimes . . . sometimes I feel scared.'

Flynn's mouth fell open. 'I'd *never* hurt you,' he said.

'Maybe not physically,' I admitted. 'But when you lose your temper, I hate it. And the truth is that it makes me doubt you, because it makes me question *everything*. It makes everything unstable *all* the time.' I took a deep breath. 'The truth, the real truth, is that I wasn't sure whether to trust you over the iPads because you're so changeable all the time.'

Flynn pressed his lips together in a thin, miserable line.

I stared back at him. This was agony.

'You mean you didn't really trust me?' he said in a dull, flat voice.

'I wanted to, I just couldn't be sure. That's what I'm saying – you're so . . . calm one minute, furious the next, it's hard to know what's real . . .' I stopped, unable to bear the terrible look of hurt on Flynn's face.

'I didn't realise you felt like . . . that.' He frowned.

'I'm just trying to be honest,' I said. A vision of me and James in the back of that taxi flashed through my head. I pushed it away – telling Flynn about that meaningless kiss would be too much honesty. He didn't need to know. 'Anyway, you and me aren't the whole story, are we?' I went on. 'What about your mum? She was the main reason you agreed to go to Ireland. Doesn't she matter anymore?'

'Of course she does,' Flynn said. 'Mum's fine. She's working less hard and loving staying with her sister. Siobhan's happy too. That guy she's with, Gary. He's okay. *More* than okay. He really cares about her. They've got this little flat near Mum. It's one of the reasons I can leave now. He's looking after Siob. And I know he'll look out for Mum too. And Cait's settled in at school.' He looked sullenly at the ground. 'It's just me. I don't fit in there.'

There was a long pause. A soft breeze ruffled my hair. I took a step away.

'You don't fit in anywhere,' I sighed. 'You don't even *try* to fit in. And you know it takes more than talent and determination to be successful. You can't do everything on your own.'

'Yes I can,' Flynn said tersely.

We stared at each other across the grass.

'No,' I said. 'Remember, back after the thing with your dad, the police and your mum and everyone said maybe you should go to see a counsellor?'

'No way,' Flynn snapped. 'Therapy's for freaks.'

Silence.

'What about your dad?' I said. 'Suppose you see him? Suppose he does something to annoy you and you lose your temper again.'

Flynn's face clouded. 'I'll handle it,' he said.

'I saw him a few weeks ago,' I blurted out.

Flynn frowned. 'Why didn't you tell me?' he growled.

'Cos I knew you'd be mad,' I said. 'Your dad followed me down the high street. Asked for some money, like you said he would.'

'What did you do? What happened?' Flynn's voice was tense.

'I told him I didn't have any,' I said. 'He knew you'd gone to Ireland, said something about you being angry . . .'

'I don't want him knowing anything about my life.' Flynn clenched his fists. 'I told you just to walk away. Not to even speak . . .'

'It wasn't like that . . . I couldn't just—'

'Yes you could, it's not safe. He could have hurt you,' Flynn shouted. He caught his breath. 'River, I'm sorry. I didn't mean to yell like that . . .'

I gazed at his face. It was always there, I realised. The anger inside him. The hate. Just bubbling away under the surface.

I couldn't live with that.

I didn't *want* to live with that.

'River?'

'I don't want to worry about whether or not you're going to fly off the handle at the least little

259

thing.' I looked him in the eyes. 'I love you. I *really* do. But I don't want to be always scared. Wondering who's going to make you mad next. Worried it'll be me . . .'

I turned away, so he wouldn't see the tears that were pricking at my eyes. I stood very still, concentrating on not crying. And then I sensed Flynn move closer to me, I couldn't hear him or see him, but I knew he was there – right behind me.

We stood in silence for a few seconds. Then I felt his fingertips on the side of my neck. I closed my eyes, shivering. He traced his fingers along my skin, scraping my hair aside.

'River.' Flynn's voice was low, pleading, his breath warm against my bare neck. My skin erupted in goosebumps. 'You have no idea how much I . . . I only want you.'

I wanted to stay there and let him kiss me. I wanted it so badly my whole body was shaking. I felt his hand on my arm.

'I want to show you that you can trust me,' he whispered, his lips soft on my neck. 'I'll change, I promise. I'll never lose my temper again.'

I could feel myself falling, falling. But for the first time I could see *where* I was falling – into a nightmare of lies to my parents and fear of Flynn getting angry.

Lies and mistrust and fear.

I dug my nails into my palms. 'Your promises are just like your apologies,' I said. 'Don't you see? You can't say you won't get angry or out of control and expect it to just happen. It's too deep down in you, too much a part of who you are . . .'

Flynn ran his hand down my arm and across my waist, pulling me into him so my back was pressed against his chest. He leaned forwards, his cheek rubbing against mine.

'Please, Riv, I can do this,' he whispered.

I nearly gave in. I swear I was so close to just turning round and kissing him like I'd never kissed him before. But something – a single, tiny thread of strength – told me that if we had a future it couldn't start like this. He had to know I meant what I said.

I pulled away from him and turned around so we were facing each other. 'I believe you can do it, too. But I don't believe you can do it without help.'

The wind swirled around us. Flynn's fringe fell over his eyes. He brushed it away with a frown.

'It has to be counselling,' I said, thinking of the anger management therapy Dad had talked about before. 'A proper effort to deal with your temper, like the police and your mum suggested.'

'You've got to be kidding, Riv.' Flynn stared at me, his eyes greener than ever in the bright sunlight. 'I'm not doing some stupid course. I don't need it for a start and—'

'It's the only way,' I interrupted. 'You know you get too angry about stuff. Like with your dad and how you hurt him. You admitted it before. It wasn't right how you felt. What you did. Maybe if you can face up to that . . .'

'Don't do this, Riv.' Flynn clenched his teeth. I could see him struggle for a second, then the roar exploded out of him. 'I freakin' love you. Why isn't that enough?'

I stared at him, my heart thumping. '*That's* why,' I said steadily.

The park was quiet all around us, just the sound of the wind in the trees and children playing in the distance. There was a long pause. I took a step away from him.

'I have to go. I've got more exams to revise for.'

His eyes glistened, boring into me.

I turned around. Took another step away. Then another. My legs were shaking and my heart was pounding but I kept on walking.

I was almost at the gate when I heard his footsteps behind me.

'River?'

I stopped and turned around.

'Okay.' His voice was low and intense.

'Okay, what?' I looked across the grass, knowing my eyes were giving away how much I wanted him.

Flynn moved closer.

'Okay, what?' I repeated, looking up at him.

'Okay, you're right.' His mouth trembled, his voice hoarse and low. 'That's why I'm getting angry. You're right and I can't bear the idea that I might lose you, that I *am* losing you.' His eyes glowed as he fixed me with his intense gaze, like I was the only person in the whole world.

'Oh, Flynn.' I could barely breathe.

He moved right up to me and ran his finger down my cheek.

'The truth is . . .' His voice cracked. 'The real truth is that I'm scared.'

'Scared of what?' I whispered.

'Of not being good enough for you.'

I hesitated, my gaze fixed on his eyes, all soulful and serious. Then I leaned against his chest, feeling him lean into me too. 'That's not what I think,' I said. 'That's not it at all. I just think you have a problem and until you . . .'

'Face up to it?' Flynn pulled away. His face was

pale and drawn. 'Get help?' He rubbed his eyes. Then he looked at me again. 'I shouldn't be putting you through all this. It's not fair.'

We stood together, not touching.

'I love you so much,' I said.

'And I want to prove that I love you,' he said, his voice steadier than before. 'I'll go to anger control classes or whatever they're called, I'll do whatever it takes.'

'Really? You mean it?'

'Yes,' Flynn said. 'I promise.' He took a step back. 'And this time I'm going to *show* you that I mean it. I'm going to earn the right to be with you, River.' He took another step away from me.

'You're going?' I said. My guts twisted.

'For now.' He gave me a sad smile. 'It's the only way to prove that I've changed.'

I stared at him. The pain I felt at the prospect of being apart from Flynn was reflected in his own eyes. And yet I knew he was right to leave.

We looked at each other for a long moment, then his sad smile deepened into an entirely charming, sexy grin that made me buckle at the knees.

'Just don't go running off with any strange boys, Riv. I'll be back for you before you know it.'

He walked off.

I watched him pass through the park gate and disappear around the corner then I stepped out of the shadows and headed home.

Alone.

The story continues . . .
in *Casting Shadows*.

SOPHIE McKENZIE

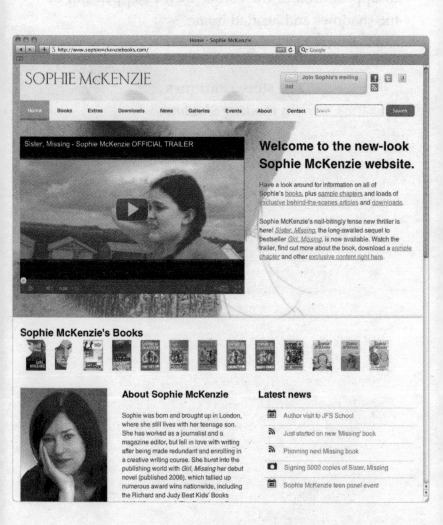

Visit
WWW.SOPHIEMCKENZIEBOOKS.COM
for news, behind the scenes articles
and exclusive book downloads.